SALLY AND THE BUTTERFLY

A pick your own path book

Written by Malaka Grant
Illustrated by Poka Studios
Edited by Ariana Murray

For my lovely children:

Nadjah, Aya, Stone and Liya

Whose bright minds and imaginations inspire my own.

Sally and The Butterfly

ISBN-13: 9781512315097

ISBN-10: 1512315095

This book is a work of fiction. Names, characters, places and incidents are either the product of the author's imagination or are used fictitiously. Any resemblance to actual events or locations of persons living or dead or yet to be born is entirely coincidental...or as the result of the (unlikely) gift of prophecy and/or divine providence.

Cover design by grantmx.

Your adventure begins now!

This book is about a little girl named Salimah. Her nickname is Sally. She is shy and sweet - sort of brave - but a little unsure of herself.

Your job is to help her complete her mission.

Throughout the pages of this book, Sally must make choices about what her next steps and decisions may be. As the adventure progresses, you will be asked questions and given instructions on which pages to turn to in order to direct Sally's quest. There are several ways this adventure can end. The power is completely in your hands.

Got it? Great. Let's get reading!

Sally's Town

In a time not too long ago, and in a town very much like yours, there lived a little girl named Sally. In Sally's Town there was a train station, a bus station and an ice-cream shop with pretty pink flowers that grew in the front window.

That's the way Sally liked to remember it.

There were lovely birds with hooked beaks that flew awkwardly from one tree to the next. Everyone had a garden and at harvest time, neighbors and friends would share the fruits and vegetables they had grown. Once in a while a deer would wander into her Town. But of all the things that lived in Sally's Town, her favorite were the butterflies.

Sadly, they did not live there anymore.

A Great Sickness had come to Sally's Town and forced everyone to stay inside their houses. No one had a name for the Sickness or knew what caused it. All they knew is that it brought great misery to the once happy people in Sally's Town. Children did not play in the streets and the grown-ups only ever went outside if it was truly necessary. In fact, the only people who dared to come into the street was the grumpy Mayor and his son, and they often drove in their huge car, kicking up dust and scaring the birds. Sally wanted to play with the Mayor's son, but Mama said that it was not allowed.

And then one day, the birds just left and the Mayor had nothing else to frighten with his big, loud engine.

For Sally, these were lonely times. On the day her mother and father left her in search of food and help, they told her to keep safe in their cozy mud and stone house. Whenever Mama and Poppa had to leave Town, they usually left Sally in the care of their elderly neighbor, Mrs. Greenwood.

"Be sure to mind Mrs. Greenwood, Salimah," her mother said while tying a soft yellow scarf over her thick, long braids. "Obey and do everything she asks you too, okay? Your father and I will be back as soon as we can."

Mama only called her 'Salimah' when something was wrong. Maybe she had done something to make her parents go away. Were they angry with her?

"No, no my darling," Sally's father whispered, scooping her up in his strong arms. "Mama and I have to find a way to help our Town. We need you to stay here..."

"And stay hidden from view," Mama added sternly.

Sally looked at the floor and tried not to cry.

"I could come with you. I could help," she whispered.

Poppa clicked his tongue and squeezed her tighter with a hug.

"You would be a better help to us here," he said. "Our job will be much easier if we knew you were safe."

Mama nodded her head and picked up her basket. She had put water, a bit of bread and a small morsel of meat in it for their journey.

"The big wide world is no place for a little child like you," Mama said. "You be a good girl for Mrs. Greenwood."

Mama narrowed her eyes and put her hand on her hip to show she meant business. Sally nodded and did not argue anymore. She liked Mrs. Greenwood because she

7

was always kind to her. Still, Sally was going to miss her parents very much; but their minds were made up. She could not go with them.

Poppa knew that Sally was sad. He was sad too. He did not want to leave her, but the Town needed help.

"I love you, Salimah," he sang. "You're my favorite girl."

"I'm your only girl!" she giggled as Poppa tickled her.

Mama stood at the door and waited. She wanted to hug Sally too, but something stopped her. Instead, she cleared her throat and tapped her right toe.

"It's time to go, Poppa," said Mama.

Sally's father set her feet on the floor and gave Sally a butterfly he had made of old faded newspaper and twigs. Sally gasped and gave her father another hug.

"Thank you, Poppa!" Sally exclaimed.

Poppa hugged her back and said, "We'll see you soon, my little butterfly!"

And then they were gone.

Sally waited every day for Mama and Poppa to come back. Soon the days turned into weeks, and those weeks turned into months. There was still no word from Mama or Poppa. Every day, Sally waited for them by the window and peered down the road until Mrs. Greenwood called her away.

"Come here and eat something, child," Mrs. Greenwood said in her croaking, old lady voice. "No use staring at the air. It won't make your parents show up no faster."

"Yes, Mrs. Greenwood."

Sally flopped onto the hard dining room chair and looked at her plate. Boiled porridge *again*. She was so sick of eating porridge that she thought she might turn into a pony! She gobbled down the warm oats and put her bowl into the sink.

"You want to help me knit a little, Sally?" asked Mrs. Greenwood kindly.

Sally looked at the window and sighed. Mrs. Greenwood was right. Staring at the air wouldn't make her parents show up any faster.

"Sure. I guess," Sally said.

"Pass me that ball of green yarn and we'll make something pretty," said Mrs. Greenwood. "What would you like to knit?"

Sally's face lit up with a smile.

"Let's make a blanket that looks like a garden!" she exclaimed. "A garden like the one I and all the other kids used to play in before..."

Sally didn't finish her sentence. She didn't have to. Mrs. Greenwood knew what Sally was going to say. She patted Sally's hand and smiled at her kindly. Sally was going to say, "before the Sickness came". So many of Sally's friends had never gotten better after they had gotten sick, and now she was almost all alone.

"A garden sounds mighty fine, Salimah. Here; let's add some red to it too. I think I remember a rose bush in that old garden."

Sally used her knitting needles after Mrs. Greenwood showed her how, and for a while, she forgot all about the Sickness, about Mama and Poppa being gone, and that her belly was rumbling because she was still very, very hungry.

The Butterfly

Howling winds whipped around the corners of Sally's small mud and stone cottage. The season was beginning to change. Soon, the Dry Season would come and what was left of all the pretty flowers would wilt, leaving parched red earth in their place until the Rains returned three months later.

Sally sat at the window just as she had done every day, waiting for Mama and Poppa to return. She rubbed her eyes and yawned. Mrs. Greenwood was napping in her favorite chair with a book on her chest. The old lady's light snoring was making Sally feel sleepy as well. Maybe she would take a nap too? Sally stood up and got ready to walk over to Poppa's favorite chair by the lamp. On cold nights, Sally used to sit in his lap while he drank his tea and read her stories from the newspaper. She missed her Poppa so very much. A nap in his chair would make her feel happy.

Just as Sally turned to walk to the comfy chair, she heard a light tapping against the window. What was that sound? Sally walked closer to investigate. There was nothing there. Sally turned away from the window and took another step toward the chair. There it was again! The tapping noise!

"What is that?" Sally wondered out loud. This time, she looked down toward the bushes that sat outside of the window sill.

Something with big wings flew straight into the window.

"Woi!" Sally screamed, stumbling over her feet. Her heart was racing wildly in her chest. Had a bird hurt itself trying to get into her house? There were no more birds in her Town. They had all flown away after the Sickness came. There was no longer any food for them here.

Sally put her hand on the door knob and prepared to go outside. Suddenly, she remembered Mama's words:

Stay in the house and be sure to mind Mrs. Greenwood.

Sally looked at Mrs. Greenwood and wondered what she should do. She was sleeping so deeply. It would be rude to wake her up right now, wouldn't it? Mrs. Greenwood loved her sleep. Sally thought about it and had an idea. She would just go outside quickly, just for a minute to see if the bird was alright. She was so confused...what was the right thing to do?

If you want Sally stay inside like her mother told her to, go to page 43

If you want Sally to go outside and investigate, go to the next page

"Hello? Are you okay?" she whispered loudly. "Please come out. I won't hurt you!"

Something rustled over to the right side of the house, where the corn fields were once planted. The field was dry and barren now. Nothing had grown there since the Sickness came to her Town. Mama and Poppa had put up a short wall made of mud blocks around the cottage to keep the animals from coming into their compound to look for food, and now something *was* trying to get in. Sally held her breath as she took gentle steps toward the sound. Her heart was pounding wildly. What if it tried to eat her?

The dry ground crunched underneath her feet as she tip-toed. She leaned as close to the wall as she dared and peeked through one eye. Nothing. Sally breathed in relief and turned to go back to her cottage. Just then something flew into her face.

"Ei! Ei! Ei!" she screamed in fright. She closed her eyes. What was this big thing? Why did it keep flying at her?

When she calmed down, she opened her eyes and looked around. Something soft was on her arm.

"What a huge butterfly!" she exclaimed.

The butterfly flapped its wings slowly. It was the biggest butterfly Sally had ever seen. Its wings were the colors of a rainbow trapped in a sunlit puddle and they glowed like a full moon. Most butterflies were only one or two colors. This was a very special butterfly. Sally decided she would keep it for herself and show Mama and Poppa when they got home.

She carefully lifted her left hand to cover the butterfly. Almost there...

Before she could catch it the butterfly flew away!

"Oh, no! Please come back," she begged.

Sally chased after the butterfly until she got to the edge of the short mud wall. The butterfly was resting on a leaf on the ground. Maybe if she tried to grab the leaf instead of the butterfly, she might have better luck. Sally inched forward until she was just over the colorful insect. She smiled.

"No you have nowhere to go, Big Butterfly!"

She leapt forward with her arms outstretched...

... and fell into a deep, dark hole.

"Woi!!! Help! Someone help me!!" Sally called.

Sally fell and fell and fell. The wind was rushing by her ears. It felt like she was in a storm! The bottom of the hole was coming. She could tell. Sally prepared to hit the ground with a thump. This was going to hurt. But suddenly, she began to float like the feathers of the white river birds that once lived in her Town, and she landed gently on her feet.

Shaken and very scared, Sally looked around. She was all alone. Who was going to find her? What was she going to do? A tear fell from her eye and she began to sob quietly in the dark.

"Please don't cry," said a sweet voice in the darkness.

"Wh-who's there?" Sally whispered. "Please tell me your name!"

"My name is Ayla," said the voice. "Welcome to Amani, Land of the Enchanted."

A faint light shone on the owner of the voice. It was the rainbow butterfly Sally had tried to capture.

17

Sally goes to Amani

"Amani? Land of the Enchanted? Where am I?" Sally had so many questions. "Why aren't we in my Town? How long has this hole been here?"

Ayla fluttered her wings gently and hovered in front of Sally's nose, sending a gentle wave of cool air over her face.

"The hole was never there, Sally," she answered. "It is a gateway to Amani, and I am the Gatekeeper. It can only be revealed if I allow it."

"So, that means you wanted me to come here?" Sally asked. Suddenly she didn't feel so afraid.

"Yes, Salimah. Amani needs you. You have work to do here," said Ayla. "Our land needs your help."

"My help?" Sally was confused. "How can I help you? And how do you know my name?"

Ayla landed on Sally's nose so that she could stare into her eyes.

"I know everything about you, Salimah. There is a power in you my dear, and that is the power that is going to free this kingdom."

Sally thought about what her mother had said just a few weeks ago. She could be a better help if she stayed at home and kept safe. The big, big world was no place for a little girl like her. Ayla was wrong. She must have had the wrong child. She shook her head and blew the butterfly off her nose.

"I think you've made a mistake," she said glumly. "I'm just a kid. I don't think there is anything I can do."

Ayla folded her arms in front of her and glared at Sally.

"If you do not come and fight for Amani, many lives will be lost, Salimah. Our kingdom has no hope without you. We have waited for your arrival for a long time."

Sally crossed her arms and glared back at Ayla.

"I'm eight years old. You couldn't have been waiting that long!" she snapped. "And no one ever calls me 'Salimah' unless I'm in trouble. I'm just plain old Sally. Am I in trouble?"

Ayla fluttered her rainbow wings gently and laughed.

"No... Sally," she replied gently. "I will make you a deal. Meet with the people of Amani. Talk to them. After you do that, then decide whether or not you think you can help us. Will you do that for me?"

Sally looked around at the small dark hole she had been standing in. Getting out seemed like a better idea than just sitting there waiting for a grown up to find her. Mrs. Greenwood never went outside and there was no telling when Mama and Poppa would be returning.

"I agree," Sally nodded. "Where's the door to get out of here?"

"There is no door," said the butterfly.

"Then how do we get out of here?" Sally asked.

"You just have to believe you will."

Ayla fluttered away from Sally and smiled at her.

"Go on," she said. "Just believe. Imagine what you think the Land of Amani might look like when you get there."

Sally closed her eyes and let her imagination take over. She thought of Ayla the Butterfly and all her bright colors. Amani must have lots of flowers, green grass and trees for butterflies to live in. It was a beautiful land. She couldn't wait to see it!

"Open your eyes, Sally," Ayla said softly. "The way is now open."

When Sally's eyes flew open she was standing in a meadow filled with sweet smelling violet petals and soft moss. Up ahead there was a curtain of leaves with light filtering through it. Sally raced towards it. She couldn't wait to see the rest of Amani! When she got to the edge of the leafy curtain, she threw it back and stepped through. She was in Amani, Land of the Enchanted! But was *nothing* like what she imagined.

A Dark Kingdom

"It's so... bleak. So dark!" Sally gasped.

She was in shock.

Where were all the flowers she had imagined? Where were the fluffy white clouds and crystal clear stream? Why, this land didn't look enchanted at all!

Sally stepped cautiously out of the tunnel to get a better look. A twig snapped beneath her feet. She yelped in surprise.

"Shhh!" Ayla said harshly. "We must be very silent until we get to safety. There may be Orbeasts about."

"What's an Orbeast?" asked Sally.

"It's a big, horrible monster," Ayla replied. Her wings suddenly didn't look so bright. She was sad. "They are different from the people of Amani. They don't belong here. But come, Sally! There's no time to discuss it now. We have to get out of this field."

Ayla fluttered her huge wings and floated towards a tree line in the distance. It looked like a dark forest.

Sally was a little afraid, but she followed Ayla, jumping over mud puddles and slimy leaves. Some of the muck stuck to her sandals. She wished she had worn better shoes. But how could she have known she was going to be chasing butterflies in a magic land when she woke up that morning?

"We're almost there!" called Ayla. "Don't give up yet!"

"I won't!" Sally grunted. She had been stuck inside her house so long because of the Sickness that she had forgotten what it felt like to run! Her lungs felt like they were burning, but the wind felt good on her soft, brown cheeks.

Soon, they reached the dense forest. The leaves and bushes in this part of Amani did not look as dry as the part Sally had just run through. This part of the forest looked like there was still life inside of it. Ayla beckoned Sally towards her.

"Through here, Sally."

Sally looked around. There was a wall of dark green leaves blocking her path.

"Through where?" she whimpered. "There's no way to get through!"

Just then, something growled in the distance. It was a deep, low sound. It sounded angry. Sally was suddenly *very* afraid.

"Come on, Sally," Ayla begged. "You have to believe you can do this!"

"But there's no way I can get through. It's a thick wall of leaves and I'm just a kid!"

The growling was getting closer and louder.

Ayla set her tiny feet on Sally's nose and flapped her wings against Sally's forehead. Her voice was calm when she spoke.

"Yes, you *are* a kid, Salimah – but that doesn't mean you don't have power. Trust yourself. You can do this."

Sally gazed at Ayla's wings and then closed her eyes. She imagined herself behind the wall and believed she was there, safe. She opened her eyes and looked around. She was still stuck in the same spot. Her heart sank as the growling and rustling got louder.

"You did it!" Ayla said proudly.

"What do you mean? We're still stuck out here!"

Sally was beginning to panic even more. Ayla floated to the bottom of the hedge and nodded her head towards a small gap.

"Look! Here's the way in. Follow me!"

Sally sprinted toward the narrow gap and slid her body in sideways. Before she could get through, something snagged the hem of her skirt. As she tugged the brown fabric, something tugged back. It was an Orbeast!

"Don't look at it, Sally!" Ayla exclaimed. "Just come through the opening...quick!"

Sally snatched her skirt out of the grasp of a leathery, scaly hand and scrambled through the leafy corridor. When she was safe, she put her hand against her chest and tried to catch her breath. When she looked up, she discovered was inside a room with red clay walls. A small ray of sunlight filtered through the ceiling. In the dimness, she could make out the shapes of animals. Had Ayla led her into a trap? Sally looked frantically around for the big butterfly. She was resting on winding, knotted root growing through a wall to the left. This was the inside of a tree!

Before Sally had the chance to inspect her surroundings further, one of the animals spoke.

"Who's this, eh?" a gruff voice asked. A furry bush dog stepped into the ray of light. He growled softly when Sally did not give an answer. "Have you led an enemy into our camp, Ayla?"

Sally was frightened. What if the bush dog tried to bite her? The big boys in her Town used to hunt them for fun. She always felt bad for the little dogs, but maybe they deserved it. This bush dog looked and sounded really mean.

"This is no enemy," said Ayla. "This is Salimah. She is here to help us."

"And how exactly is this skinny girl going to help us?" asked the Dog. "She almost got captured by an Orbeast just now! She can't even help herself!"

Sally reached for one of the black braids Mrs. Greenwood had platted in her hair that morning and twirled it around her finger. The dog was right. What was she thinking? How had she let the butterfly convince her that she could change anything, especially in a place as dangerous as Amani? Ayla saw that Sally was beginning to doubt herself again. Her wings flashed bright blue when she spoke.

"You don't know what strength Salimah has within her," she said sternly to the Bush Dog. "She has promised to try to help us reclaim our land, and we are going to give her the chance to live up to her promise!"

Sally looked around the room for a place to sit. There was a patch of palm leaves in the corner. They looked like the kind that Mama and the other mothers in her Town used to make brooms with. She settled on them and rested her feet. Suddenly, her palm brushed up against something cold and hard.

"Very well," the Dog grumbled. "But I won't be held responsible if anything happens to her!"

"I believe in you," the cold thing croaked. It was a tortoise.

"Why should you?" Sally muttered. "The Dog is right. I almost got myself captured. I almost let the Orbeast in here, and..."

"Yes. It's true. You *almost* did," the Tortoise said in a slow, strong voice. "But you didn't. You escaped. You got away safely. And I believe before the end is here, you will help make our land safe again."

But Sally was still very afraid. She wasn't sure what to do!

If you want Sally to ask Ayla to lead her back home, go to page 48

If you want Sally to gather courage and help the Animals of Amani, go to page 51

If you want to see the Orbeast Cave, go to the next page

The Orbeast King's Cave

The Cave of the Orbeasts was dark and stank of rotting filth and kerosene. Only the faintest rays of sunlight filtered into the dwelling. The Orbeasts did not like the sun. They did not like brightness or color, but they knew there was power in it. That is why they had come to Amani – to expand their kingdom and make more room for themselves. But the only way to do that was to destroy all the color from Amani. It was brightness and color that gave Amani its hope and joy!

San Boni, the King of the Orbeasts looked down on the patrol that had just returned to the cave. His had a evil scowl on his face.

"Did you capture the Butterfly?" he growled.

"No, my lord," said his captain. His voice was gruff, like steel wool scraping a dirty pan. "She eluded us again."

"You have failed me again!" San Boni roared. "If you can't do the job, then I will find someone who can!"

The captain of the guard lowered his head. He did not want to lose his position leading the army. Somehow, he had to prove that he was worthy of the job. As the King

of the Orbeasts paced around the cold stone floor he sneered and called for a servant to bring him a goblet.

A Tree Toad with a tray hopped over and quivered as San Boni snatched the drink and flicked him away with his clawed foot. He was not pleased. The only way to remove hope and joy from Amani was to capture the Ayla the Butterfly. She was the key!

The captain of the Orbeast Patrol spoke again saying, "There is something else, Your Highness. When Ayla the A Tree Toad with a tray hopped over and quivered as one of the Orbeasts paced around the cold stone floor he sneered and called for a servant to bring him a goblet.

San Boni snatched the drink and flicked him away with his clawed foot. He was not pleased. The only way to remove hope and joy from Amani was to capture the Ayla the Butterfly. She was the key!

The captain of the Orbeast Patrol spoke again saying, "There is something else, Your Highness. When Ayla the Butterfly came back from the Other World, she came back with a girl. She might be dangerous."

San Boni threw his head back and roared with laughter. "A girl? What can a girl do? Just go and get me that Butterfly and don't return until you do!"

You may go back to page 31 to make another choice for Sally

Sally meets the Orbeast Prince

"Your Majesty! We've caught her! We've caught the girl!"

A scaly hand threw Sally to the ground in front of a throne made of wood, leather and iron. Sally looked up slowly and saw massive green feet, thin bony knees, a broad chest with a shield on it and then finally, the face of a young Orbeast. Sally was surprised.

"Ei! How possible? You're nothing but a kid...like me!" she gasped.

The Orbeast Soldier who had dragged her into the throne room smacked Sally across the cheek.

"Mind your tone when you're talking to Tolu, Prince of the Orbeasts!" he growled. "Show some respect!"

Prince Tolu raised his hand and signaled for his soldier to leave Sally alone.

"There is no need to be so rough with her, now that we have her in our clutches," he said quietly.

Sally was surprised. Why was this Orbeast being so kind?

"Send word to my father in the Mountain Caves. Tell him that we have captured a prisoner. I will personally make sure you will all be rewarded for your hard work."

The Orbeasts Patrol grunted and growled with glee, happy that they would receive gifts from the hand of the Prince himself. They bowed and left Prince Tolu and Salimah alone in the throne room. Prince Tolu walked slowly towards Sally. The claws of his large feet scratched the stone floor. Sally scrambled to her feet and backed away from him.

"Don't be afraid," he said quietly. Prince Tolu's voice was low and growly, just like the other Orbeasts...but his seemed kinder. "What is your name?"

"I won't tell you," Sally said defiantly.

"Well, that's not fair," Prince Tolu chuckled. "You know my name, so I should know yours. It's only polite.

Was this Orbeast trying to make friends with her? How could she know she could trust him? Prince Tolu was smiling, or at least that's what his lips pressed against sharp, yellow teeth looked like they were doing. Sally decided to trust him and told him her name.

"Sally is my nickname. It's short for 'Salimah'."

"And where do you come from?" Prince Tolu asked. He seemed very interested.

"I don't know. I come from Town," Sally replied slowly. "It's hard to explain. I came through a hole under a wall while I was chasing a Butterfly."

"You mean you're from the Other World?"

Prince Tolu's eyes got very wide. Suddenly, Sally was very afraid. She had said too much! Ayla had already said the Orbeasts would be looking for her...to destroy her. Would Prince Tolu force her to lead him to Sally at the Tree Fortress?

When Sally didn't reply, he knew he was right. He grabbed her by the hand and pulled her to her feet.

"Come with me," he growled.

"Where are you taking me?" Sally shouted.

Prince Tolu put his large hand over her mouth and told her to keep quiet.

"I'm going to help you," he whispered. "Now don't make a sound and follow me!"

He led her through a maze of tunnels, one turning into a smaller one and then a bigger one. Sally felt sick and dizzy from the putrid smell and the darkness.

"Where are we?" she whispered.

"We are in the bedrock underneath the River in the west," Prince Tolu said softly. "The River..."

"...feeds the Tree Fortress!" Sally said excitedly. "But why are you taking me there?"

Prince Tolu stopped and looked at Sally with big, sad eyes.

"I never wanted to come to Amani," he said. "But my father is greedy. All he cares about is power, land and wealth. I've seen how his actions make the lands we conquer so miserable. I want to help stop it if I can."

"But if you help me, that means you'll have to go against your father's wishes," said Sally. "I was taught that we must always obey our elders!"

"I believe that too," nodded Prince Tolu. "But my father's actions are wicked...and they are not helping others. I have to make this choice, just like I know you had to make choice in coming to Amani. I will help you any way I can."

Prince Tolu led Sally to the mouth of the dam, where the waters of the River had been plugged up.

"How do I release it?" she asked nervously. She was beginning to lose confidence!

Prince Tolu was already heading back into the tunnels. He was going to free the rest of the Animals the Orbeast Patrol had captured.

"You have to figure it out on your own, Sally!" he called. "You have to be smart, and believe in yourself!"

And then he was gone, and once again Sally was all alone. It was all up to her now. Sally did not want to be alone.

"I wish you were here with me, Ayla," she whispered in the dark.

Just then, a familiar light appeared in the gloom. Could it really be her friend, the Butterfly? It was!

"I would never leave you alone, Salimah," Ayla said. "I had hoped that Prince Tolu would be an ally, and by his actions today, he has proven that he will be a good king one day. Hopefully he can teach the other Orbeasts his ways."

Sally nodded. She was so happy to see Ayla that she didn't know what to say.

"Hurry, Sally! We have no time to waste," said Ayla, fluttering her wings quickly. "We have to get to the top of the River dam now!"

To see what happens next, turn to page 68

Sally Decides to stay inside

No. She couldn't do it. It would be wrong to disobey her mother. Imagine how disappointed she would be if Mrs. Greenwood informed her parents that she had gone outside after they told her not to!

Sally took her hand off the doorknob and sat back down in Poppa's big comfy chair. She looked at a stack of old magazines and books and thought about reading them. Most of them were older than she was. When Mama had a shop outside of their house selling groundnuts, she would carefully tear the pages from the magazines and wrap them up for their customers.

Now there were no more groundnuts and no more customers. Sally had read each page of those old magazines again and again.

Tap

Tap

Tap!

Ah. There was that sound again! The poor bird must have been desperate to get into the house. The noise roused Mrs. Greenwood from her sleep.

"Is that you making that noise, Salimah?" she asked.

"No, Mrs. Greenwood," Sally replied. "I think there is a bird beating against the window."

Mrs. Greenwood stood up and brushed the wrinkles from her long skirt.

"Come," she said, taking Sally's hand, "let's take a look."

As they approached the dusty window pane, Sally shrieked with delight.

"It's a butterfly! A beautiful butterfly!"

Mrs. Greenwood frowned. Sally asked her why she wasn't smiling. Was she not happy to see the butterfly?

"Oh yes, I am! Very happy," Mrs. Greenwood replied. "But there are no more plants or flowers in our Town to attract butterflies. I wonder why it is here."

Sally nodded her head and was reminded again about how the Sickness had taken all the beauty from her

Town. Her lip began to tremble, but she forced herself not to cry. Mrs. Greenwood saw that Sally was upset, so she put her hand around her shoulder and told her a story about when she was a little girl growing up in Town. She told Sally about the big shady trees, the cool pools of water, and the traders that would walk up and down the road from other villages to sell their wares.

"We had many animals that lived here," Mrs. Greenwood smiled. "But the butterflies were very few. I chased one once, and it led me to a lovely garden that I never knew existed!"

Sally was amazed. As Mrs. Greenwood described the garden, she felt a longing to go there and see it for herself.

"Did the butterfly you chased look anything like this one?" Sally asked hopefully.

"Yes. In fact, it did," Mrs. Greenwood replied with another frown. "It looked exactly like this one."

By this time, the Butterfly had perched on the window sill, watching the old woman and the little girl talk about her. Sally thought the butterfly wanted her to come outside, but she could not be sure. It was so beautiful...and big! The biggest butterfly she had ever seen. Mrs. Greenwood recognized the look in Sally's eyes. She knew the little girl wanted to get closer to the magnificent insect.

"Ahhh, Sally! You want to go outside eh?"

"Yes Auntie Greenwood, I do."

Mrs. Greenwood pulled Sally closer and whispered to her.

"I will let you go outside for 10 minutes, but no longer than that. When I call for you, you must come back!"

Sally was suddenly afraid. She wanted to go, but she also remembered her promise to her mother. Now Mrs. Greenwood was giving her a choice. What should she do?

If you want Sally to go outside to see the Butterfly, go to page 15

If you want Sally to stay inside, stay on this page and keep reading.

Sally shook her head and sat by the fireplace.

"No," she said. "I will just sit inside like Mama told me to."

Sally picked up the yarn for the blanket Mrs. Greenwood was knitting with before her nap. She asked her if she wanted to continue making their blanket. Mrs. Greenwood smiled and nodded, and took her seat. Her needles began clicking away as she began to knit roses to decorate the blanket.

Tap

Tap

Tap!

The Butterfly tapped the window a few more times. But when Sally looked back at the window, it was gone.

-The End-

Sally misses her home

Salimah cleared her throat and looked at Ayla. A tear dropped slowly from her eye. She felt she was not smart or strong enough to defeat the Orbeasts.

"Ayla," she begged. "Please lead me back home. I can't do this..."

The Dog growled in mockery, saying, "See? I told you. We've wasted enough time on this human girl!"

Ayla looked very sad as well, but she knew she could not force Sally to feel stronger than she felt. She had to develop courage on her own. Ayla floated down to Sally's shoulder and whispered to her.

"I can't lead you back, Sally," she said softly. "I took a big risk coming to get you from the Other World. By now the Orbeast Patrol will be out looking for me."

"But if you can't lead me back...who can?" Sally asked. She was very worried.

"Don't worry," Ayla replied assuredly. "The Hummingbirds will guide you. But you must run swiftly to keep up with them!"

Sally noticed again that the brightness in Ayla's wings had begun to fade even more. She now looked colorless and nearly gray.

"What will you do, now that I am going?" Sally asked. "I thought you said I was your only hope."

"Don't worry about us, Salimah," Ayla replied, forcing a smile. "As long as I am alive, there is hope in Amani. Now, go! Quickly!"

Sally followed the Hummingbird family through a small, secret opening in the largest bough of the Tree Fortress and raced after the small birds. Their wings flapped so fast that they seemed to disappear from view! Poppa Hummingbird tweeted loudly at Sally, urging her to hurry.

"There's a dust cloud ahead!" he yelled. "We must run around it!"

Sally picked up her pace and ran as quickly as she could. The red dust was beginning to blind her, making her cough and choke. She ran in a wide circle, following the Hummingbirds flight pattern. Suddenly, Baby Hummingbird stopped in fear.

"That's not a dust cloud," he chirped. "It's the Orbeast Patrol!"

Sally stopped running too, and dropped to the ground in total dread. What had she done! She should have stayed with Ayla. She should have stayed home with Mrs. Greenwood! What could she do next?

To see what happens to Sally, go to page 73

Sally helps to defend Amani

Sally knew Amani could be as beautiful as she imagined it. She wanted to help. Sally gathered her courage and promised to help defend the Animals of Amani, no matter what it took.

Within the safety of the Tree Fortress, Ayla called all Amani's animal forces together to plan their defense strategy. The old Tortoise sat in the center of the gathering and folded his feet to his side, laying perfectly still. Ayla hovered above the Tortoise and unfurled her majestic wings so that they caught the fading sunlight. Sally gasped as a map of the land of Amani materialized on his old, scaly shell.

"The Tree Fortress is as the center of the land," said a Humming Bird. "The Orbeast have already captured the River to the west, the Sand Dunes to the north, the Flower Fields to the east and the Mountains in the south."

"So we're surrounded," Sally muttered. "It's completely hopeless!"

The Bush Dog shook his head and growled, "It's not hopeless so long as the Tree Fortress remains free! It is the heart of Amani, and holds all its powers."

"He's right," Ayla said weakly. "As long as the Tree Fortress stands, the life of Amani will remain safe."

Ayla did not look well. The color in her wings was growing dimmer and dimmer. Sally was very concerned for her.

"Ayla...what else are you not telling me?" Sally had a sudden idea and scooted closer to the Tortoise before asking her next question. "Are you the key to all this?"

"I am the Guardian of Amani," Ayla replied. "As long as I am alive and safe, Hope and Joy will remain in our land."

Sally peered at Ayla's wings. They were far more colorful now!

"Your wings! They're beginning to glow again."

A Fawn emerged from the shadows, her eyes bright with faith. She nudged Sally's hand with her soft, wet nose to get her attention.

"Ayla was right to come and get you," she said in a hushed voice. "She said as long as someone from the Other World believed in the magic of Amani – believed in Hope and Joy – our kingdom would be saved!"

This made Sally feel much more confident. She squared her shoulders and dusted her hands. She was ready to do her part to save Amani.

"What do we do next?" she asked, peering at the map on the Tortoise's back. "What's our plan?"

There was only ONE way to stop the Orbeasts. Someone had to get to the River in the west and unplug the dam the Orbeast had built. The River fed the mighty Tree Fortress...all green things need water to live. There was just enough water in the trunks of the old tree to keep it alive, but the Animals of Amani did not know for how much longer.

The Bush Dog sat up on his haunches, sniffed the air and howled.

"What do you smell, Bush Dog?" asked the Fawn, fearing the worst.

"The Orbeasts have returned, and they are very close," he growled. "Someone must stay and defend the Tree Fortress while the others leave for the River!"

If you want Sally to stay and defend the Tree Fortress, go to the next page

If you want Sally to leave and help unplug the River, go to page 65

Sally stays to help fight the Orbeasts

The Orbeast Patrol was getting closer and closer. Their enormous feet beat the ground, making a thicker and thicker cloud of dust. There was little time to come up with a plan. Sally and the Animals of Amani would have to rely on their quick wits.

"Gather anything that can be used to defend the Tree Fortress," Sally yelled. "They may come with axes and knives. We have to be ready!"

Ayla fluttered to the different animal groups, giving instructions. She told the Fawn, the Ostriches and the Gazelles to run ahead to the River because they were the fastest. She told the Tortoise, the Bush Dog and the Jackals to stay with her at the Tree Fortress, because they were the strongest.

Sally saw a vine at the top of the tree and began to climb it.

"Where is she going?" the Bush Dog growled. "She's scared! She's hiding!"

"We don't have time to worry about that now," replied Ayla. "Get to the surface. Get ready to defend!"

56

The Orbeasts had come so close to the line of defense! The Animals of Amani lined up, blocking the entrance to the Tree Fortress from the invaders. Soon, Animals and Orbeasts were growling, snarling and biting. Sally sat above the fighting, climbing from bough to bough until she found what she was looking for: a cluster of baobab fruits.

Sally began to hurl them from the trees, knocking Orbeasts in their heads, causing them to be dizzy and collapse. She was surprised at how accurate her aim was! Soon, the Baboon Troop that had been hiding from the fighting joined her as well. They grabbed the meaty fruit, smashing it into the heads and bodies of the Orbeasts. The Orbeasts did *not* like the sticky juices on their scaly skins. They snarled and tried to figure out a way to get to Sally in the branches of the Tree.

Ayla floated up to Sally's spot in the branches, with wings shining brighter and more colorful with each passing moment. She perched on the tip of Sally's nose.

"It's time, Sally!" Ayla shouted above the noise. "You've proven that you are brave, strong, and full of courage! Get ready!"

"Time for what?" Sally yelled back. "Get ready for what?"

In that instant, Sally felt a strange sensation wash over her. It was like the shimmer of cold rain and felt tingly, like the mint tea the old men in the Town drank on hot afternoons. Sally lost her footing on the tree branch she was standing on, but she didn't fall. She was flying!

How could this be?

Sally looked behind her and saw that Ayla had connected her body with hers.

"Your strength made mine stronger, Salimah, and it made me so glad," Ayla explained, flapping her majestic, delicate wings. "And now we are connected by Hope and Joy."

"But where are we going?" Sally said. She was concerned for the animals they had left behind in battle.

"We have to get to the River in the west," Ayla explained. "Don't worry. The Bush Dog and the Tortoise can hold that lot off!"

Sally looked down over Amani, and saw how parched and brown the earth was. There was no life in it. The Orbeasts had stolen almost all of it! She was angry...and determined.

"Faster Ayla! Get us to that River!"

To go to the River, go to page 67

Sally Finds Home

Sally felt very calm like she was being carried by bubbles, soft sand and clouds. It was like floating in a dream.

Suddenly, she heard someone calling her name.

Sally! Sally! Salimah! Wake up, my sweet heart!

Sally looked around and saw the concerned faces of Mama, Poppa and Mrs. Greenwood. She wiped her forehead, which was wet with sweat and water. She jumped when she saw everyone staring at her.

"Where am I?" she gasped.

"You're at home in your bed," Poppa chided. "Where else would you be?"

"You've been asleep for hours," Mrs. Greenwood said. "You missed your mummy and daddy coming home. They brought help...medicine and food!"

Sally looked around at her house, not sure that it was all real. There was the stack of old books, and Poppa's comfy chair. Yes. It was her house! Something wonderful was cooking on the stove. She took a deep breath and inhaled the sweet smell. Mama was boiling ripe plantain and soup. Sally's stomach growled. She was starving!

"Mrs. Greenwood told us you went outside, even though we told you not to," Mama said sternly. "I'm very disappointed in you."

"Sorry, Ma," Sally said sadly.

Poppa took Sally up in his strong arms and hugged her tightly. He gave her a big kiss on the cheek.

"But she also told us she brought you in the house just in time. It started raining while you were outside." Poppa laughed. "You see, my little butterfly? You brought us rain!

Sally crinkled her forehead and tried to figure it out. How *had* the rains come to her Town? It was not the season for it. Could Ayla have had something to do with it? That must be it! Sally had saved Amani and her own Town!

Sally began to explain. "I was chasing a big butterfly, a butterfly as big as a crow when I suddenly fell into a different world..."

Mama held up her hand and told Sally to keep silent. She didn't want to hear any of that nonsense.

"You are very hungry, Salimah," she scoffed. "Eat something, and let's not hear anything more about butterflies as big as birds, eh?"

Poppa encouraged Sally to go to the dinner table and have some food. She would feel better once she had eaten, and then she could tell them the whole story. Sally could tell from their faces that they would not believe her. Mama sat by Sally to make sure she ate all her food. Mrs. Greenwood got up to leave. Now that she knew Sally was safe, she could go back to her own home.

"I finished our blanket, Salimah," said Mrs. Greenwood as she tied her scarf on her head. "It's by the window."

Mrs. Greenwood opened the door and walked out into the pouring rain. She danced and sang in the warm drops. Inside the house, Sally picked up the blanket Mrs.

Greenwood had knitted and gasped. In the center, there was a huge tree, a River to the west, the Sand Dunes to the north, the Flower Fields to the east and the Mountains in the south.

"It's Amani, land of the Enchanted!" Sally whispered to herself.

"What's that you said?" asked Poppa, looking over her shoulder.

"Nothing, Daddy," Sally replied. "I just said it was beautiful."

-The End-

Sally runs with the fastest Animals of Amani

Ayla had split the Animal groups up. She told Sally to run with the Fawn, the Gazelles and the Ostriches.

"You will have to be swift to keep up with them," Ayla warned. "They are our fastest runners in Amani."

Sally nodded and tightened the straps of her sandals. How was she going to keep up with an Ostrich, she wondered. No time to figure it out! Her four and two legged companions were off in a flash. Sally jogged behind them, but she was losing ground. She felt so defeated! Suddenly, she heard Ayla's voice in her head.

Believe, Sally. You can do this!

She could do it. She could do it! Sally ran faster and faster, running past the Fawn, jumping like the Gazelles and overtaking the Ostriches! She had never felt so wild and free before. Her feet pounded the clay earth, leaving girl-shaped footprints in the mud.

In her excitement, she forgot to pay attention to what was ahead. Sally looked up, but did not stop in time. She crashed right into the back of a huge Orbeast.

The impact made her dizzy, and she fell to the ground, covered in mud and sweat. She closed her eyes and fainted.

To find out what happens to Sally next, go to page 36

Sally gets to the top of the Dam

"I see it! I can see the top of the dam!"

Ayla and Sally reached the top of the dam and looked around for an Orbeast on guard. There was one, but he was fast asleep with his feet in the cool river water. Sally put a finger to her lips to motion for quiet. Ayla fluttered her wings, looking for a lever to release the water.

They couldn't find it anywhere!

"There's only one place it could be if we don't see it out here," Ayla whispered loudly. She looked around and listened.

The River sounded so loud and angry. It wanted to be released, not held back by the concrete, iron and wood that the Orbeasts had trapped it behind! Sally heard it too. They both looked at the sleeping Orbeast. The lever was under *him*. Oh no!

"How are we going to get him up?" Sally asked. The Orbeast guard looked so heavy!

"There's only one way," Ayla said determinedly. "We'll have to ask him politely."

"What?" cried Sally. "Ayla...wait!"

Ayla floated over to the Orbeast and perched on his nose, tapping him on his forehead.

"Excuse me? Mr. Orbeast? Could you please get up for a moment?" she said loudly.

Wha --- wha ---WHAT?!?

This Orbeast Soldier was not used to getting visitors at his guard post. Startled, he shrieked and fell head first into the pool of water.

"Now, Sally! Pull the lever and release the River now!"

Sally sprinted on her tip toes and reached for the mighty red lever, pulling it up and releasing the River's waters. The River waters sighed and rushed down into Amani, Land of the Enchanted. Sally and Ayla watched happily as the water began to wash and nourish everything it touched.

But where was the Orbeast?

"Help. Help me, please! Please help!"

She looked around and saw the Orbeast guard, struggling to swim against the tide of the rushing waters. He looked so helpless and frightened. Was it possible that not all Orbeats were bad? Sally couldn't let him drown. She had to save him!

The Orbeast's spear was still sitting next to the ground where he had been napping before. Sally grabbed it and stuck it into the water next to the soldier, telling him to grab it.

"Pull yourself out!" Sally shouted. "Pull!"

Ayla perched on the edge of Sally's nose, waving her antennae frantically.

"What are you doing, Sally? Just leave him!" Ayla yelled.

"I can't! It's my choice, and I choose to help him!"

Finally, after what seemed like an eternity, Sally managed to pull the Orbeast from the swirling water. He was dripping wet, and shivering. He pulled his lips back against his sharp, yellow teeth. He was smiling. Sally smiled back.

"Thank you, little girl," he growled.

"You're welcome," Sally replied, still smiling

The Orbeast tiptoed close to Sally and growled in her ear. "You should have left me in the water though!"

To Sally's surprise and to Ayla's horror, he gave a beastly roar and kicked her into the River!

"Salimah! No!"

Ayla dove after her, but it was too late. Sally had already disappeared under the water. Ayla searched for hours, but there was no sign of her young friend anywhere.

"I hope she remembers to be strong, and to believe in herself," the Butterfly whispered to herself sadly. Then Ayla took to the air and flew to the Tree Fortress to tell the animals how Sally bravely freed the River from the wicked Orbeast.

...But where was Sally? **Go to page 61.**

A Dusty Road Home

Sally had no strength left in her. She fell to the ground and lay there, waiting for the Orbeast Patrol to take her.

But no one touched her.

Sally's body felt achy and hot, and her heart was beating so fast she could hear it in her ears. Sally's eyes had been shut tight. She opened them slowly and looked around. She was back at the mud and stone wall outside of her home!

Crawling on her knees, she ran her hand along the base of the wall looking for an entrance back into the tunnel that Ayla had led her down. There was no trace of it anywhere! How could this be?

Suddenly, Sally heard someone yelling her name.

"Salimah! Where have you been?"

It was Mama! Sally rushed into her arms and gave her the tightest hug, rubbing dust and twigs into her cotton skirt.

"Oh, Mama! I've missed you so much," Sally cried. "And where is Poppa? Is he home too?"

Mama was about to scold Sally, but when she saw the tears streaming down her little girl's face, she softened.

"I've missed you too, Sally," Mama said, giving her a squeeze. "But what were you doing out here?"

Suddenly, Sally remembered the terror she had felt while she was being chased by the Orbeast troop. But she also remembered how exhilarated she felt, running faster than all the swiftest animals in Amani.

She grinned and pulled Mama towards the house. "Come inside, Mama! I'll tell you everything!"

Mrs. Greenwood was sitting in her seat by the fireplace, knitting just like she was when Sally had left her. She was patting Poppa's hand kindly.

"Oh, now don't be too angry with the child," she croaked. "If there is anyone you should be angry with, it's me! I gave her the choice to go outside."

Mrs. Greenwood looked at Salimah kindly and said, "It's not good to keep children indoors. Sometimes they need a little adventure!"

Sally gasped. Mrs. Greenwood must have known all about Amani!

Sally began to chatter quickly, telling her parents all about the great tree which was the Heart of Amani, about the talking animals, and about a beautiful butterfly that had begged her to rescue the land.

"But I was so frightened, Poppa," Sally said sadly. "I was supposed to help bring hope and water back into their kingdom, but didn't think I was strong or brave enough to do it."

Mama and Poppa looked at each other with concern. Sally could tell from their faces that they didn't believe her. Only Mrs. Greenwood smiled and nodded at her encouragingly.

"It's all true, Poppa, honestly!" Sally wanted her parents to believe her, but their doubtful looks made her doubt herself. Suddenly she heard Ayla's voice, telling her to believe in herself. Sally stopped talking and waited for her parents to say something...anything!

Just then, there was a tap at the window.

Tap!

Tap!

Tap!

Everyone looked at the window with astonished faces.

"Rain!" Mama gasped. "But it hasn't rained here for months...How is this possible? How is it raining now?" She stared at Sally in amazement.

Poppa picked Salimah up and swung her in the air.

"It seems like your little excursion outside brought us some good luck after all," he laughed.

Sally joined her father in laughter and pulled her parents towards the door.

"Come on! Let's go play in the rain!"

Sally looked around for Mrs. Greenwood, but the kindly old lady had already left. There, but the fireplace, was a newly knitted blanket with a huge butterfly that looked *very* similar to Ayla. Sally grinned and rushed outside to join her parents in the sweet-smelling rain.

-The End-

Dear Reader,

Did you like Salimah's adventure? Did you wish there were things she could have done differently? Well, we're in luck, because the next few pages are for you!

Write or draw your own ending to Sally and Ayla's adventure using the blank pages provided. Discuss your thoughts with your friends and family. Together, you can share ideas on other ways to save Amani from the Orbeasts or cure the Sickness in Sally's town.

We would love to hear from you when you're done! Have a grown up contact us on Twitter at @SATBFLY or on Sally's Instagram page at SATBFLY to share your pictures and stories with other readers. We can't wait to see what you creations you come up with!

CREATE YOUR OWN ADVENTURE HERE

CREATE YOUR OWN ADVENTURE HERE

CREATE YOUR OWN ADVENTURE HERE

CREATE YOUR OWN ADVENTURE HERE

Made in the USA
Middletown, DE
16 October 2016

A
FAITH
TO DIE FOR
Your Roadmap to Hope

MARK GEPPERT
Foreword by Dr Jay Passavant

GENESIS

Produced by Genesis Books
An imprint of ARMOUR Publishing Pte Ltd
Kent Ridge Post Office
P. O. Box 1193, Singapore 911107
Email: mail@armourpublishing.com
Website: www.armourpublishing.com

ISBN 981-4138-38-x

Printed in Singapore

To
Noonan

Contents

"I Send You"

"A Faith to Die For"

Psalm 56

Prayer for Relief from Tormentors

To the Chief Musician. Set to "The Silent Dove in Distant Lands."
A Michtam of David when the Philistines captured him in Gath.

[1] *Be merciful to me, O God, for man would swallow me up;*
Fighting all day he oppresses me.
[2]*My enemies would hound me all day,*
For there are many who fight against me, O Most High.
[3]*Whenever I am afraid, I will trust in You.*
[4]*In God (I will praise His word),*
In God I have put my trust; I will not fear.
What can flesh do to me?
[5]*All day they twist my words;*
All their thoughts are against me for evil.
[6]*They gather together,*
They hide, they mark my steps,
When they lie in wait for my life.
[7]*Shall they escape by iniquity?*
In anger cast down the peoples, O God!
[8]*You number my wanderings;*
Put my tears into Your bottle; Are they not in Your book?
[9]*When I cry out to You,*
Then my enemies will turn back;
This I know, because God is for me.

¹⁰*In God (I will praise His word),*
In the LORD (I will praise His word),
    ¹¹*In God I have put my trust;*
I will not be afraid. What can man do to me?
    ¹²*Vows made to You are binding upon me, O God;*
I will render praises to You,
    ¹³*For You have delivered my soul from death.*
Have You not kept my feet from falling,
That I may walk before God
In the light of the living?

Foreword

M ANY have asked the question in more reflective moments, "What can one man do to change the world"?

If you have any doubt that one man, through radical obedience to the lordship of Jesus Christ can change the world, you need to read "A Faith to Die For" by my friend and partner in ministry for twenty years, Mark Geppert.

This book reads almost like a Robert Ludlum spy novel, but in this case the characters are real and the events actually happened.

You may wonder how one man with very little resource can literally travel to some of the most remote and exotic places in the world, often with nothing more than a plane ticket and a passport, only to see God open incredible doors of opportunity every step along the way. The reason is that Mark has one simple principle upon which he has built his life, and that is that *you can trust Jesus to fulfill His Word to you.*

And though there won't be many of us that will be called to the exotic destinations or life-threatening situations that Mark finds himself in, we all face the challenges of living an obedient life wherever God has placed us in the world.

That's the value of "A Faith to Die For" for the everyday reader. It reminds us that God is with us, revealing His power and grace through us to a world that needs us even when they don't know it!

As I read Mark's book, I was appreciative of the insight

that it provided for me living in the age in which we find culture and religion increasingly in the news. By helping us understand the heart and mindset of those of other faiths and cultures, Mark helps us all to believe that God can use us in the most extreme of circumstances that we may face even if it would be with the neighbor next door, a fellow student, a co-worker, or a national statesman.

Read this book and find that God is intimately involved in your daily journey and begin to expect that the mundane can become the miraculous, a daily journey can become a life-long adventure, because that's the testimony of Mark Geppert and the purpose of God for each and every one of us.

There will be moments when we will wonder what we might do next. We question whether or not there really is an answer to our predicament, or fear that hope may be gone. It is then that we will discover, as Mark does on a multitude of occasions, that we serve a God who "never fails us or forsakes us".

What can one man do to change the world? As the hymn writer put it, "Trust and Obey, For There's No Other Way ..." or in the words of Jesus, "In this world you will have tribulation, but take heart, I have overcome the world". In this volume, you will learn how you can "take heart"; you can change the world!

Dr Jay Passavant, Senior Pastor
North Way Christian Community

Preface

IN hamlets and cities around the world a drama is unfolding. At first we see it from a distance, and then very close up and personal. Leaders tell us that it is not an "ideological struggle." They insist that militant militias are not driven by religion. "Arab" has replaced "Moslem" and "local" has replaced "Christian" in the jargon of globalization.

Where does the Christian fit in the new millennium? Is there a place for the faith that has carried billions forward for twenty centuries?

This is my fourth book. The first talks about the power of prayer for the nations. The second discusses a new management strategy in the influence of the emergence of the information generation. The third reestablishes the bedrock principles that saw us through the era of mechanization, industrialization and, now, information.

This book was written in Lhasa, Tibet. I had to wait for two weeks for the government of the Tibet Autonomous Region and the People's Republic of China to sign the three-year extension of our contract for the Survey and Treatment of Congenital Heart Disease. This has again made me a captive in a situation I could not control. Since our publisher, Armour, had been pressing for a "testimony book", I put the time to good use... I wrote.

This book shares with you a true story of capture, questioning, and blacklisting by a nation we dearly love. At present I cannot return to Indonesia. The most recent failed attempt brought the explanation, "If you come, they will kill you. We cannot protect you and we do not need a dead American in the streets of Jakarta."

I have been advised as to the dangers that await me if this story is told in full, so I have changed a few names along the way. There is already a "fatwa" extended against Christian Americans, so any further threat is redundant.

That having been said, it is my hope that, through this book, you gain a sense of step-by-step growth in faith. We are all looking for hope, belief, action, purpose and a faith for which we would be willing to commit our lives. Some do that in selfishness, living for their own gain until they die. Others go to the extreme of a monastic lifestyle in the hope of service to others. Between these twin towers dwells the bulk of the world's population. We want to know our place and purpose. We follow those who purport a way of hope. We are influenced to faith or cynicism as their overtures become symphonies and the melody line is revealed and repeated.

As with many testimony books, you will often wonder how these things could be the experience of one person. I have to say, in reading the manuscript, that Jesus has brought us on an amazing journey since that July morning when He called to me saying, "I am calling you to preach My gospel to the nations." I thank God for a wonderful wife and partner in the journey and two great sons who are serving Him today.

I also want to thank those faithful friends with whom we have shared these adventures and the churches and individuals who have paid the way. We are a team. A team that believes we do have a voice in this time to which we have been born.

Sometimes that voice has not been well received. But, for the most part, I have to say that the multitude is still hungry to hear the message that gives purpose to life. They are waiting in those hamlets and cities to receive the hope that will not fail. They are waiting to hear the Name in whom we have hope not only for this life, but for the life to come.

God has a Son. His Name is Jesus. He died for you. He is coming again to take you to a wonderful place which He has prepared for you. This is the message; we are His messengers in the earth.

Mark Geppert

"Multitudes, Multitudes in the Valley of Decision"

Matthew 9:35-38

[35]Then Jesus went about all the cities and villages, teaching in their synagogues, preaching the gospel of the kingdom, and healing every sickness and every disease among the people. [36]But when He saw the multitudes, He was moved with compassion for them, because they were weary and scattered, like sheep having no shepherd. [37]Then He said to His disciples, "The harvest truly is plentiful, but the laborers are few. [38]Therefore pray the Lord of the harvest to send out laborers into His harvest."

Matthew 14:14-21

[14]And when Jesus went out He saw a great multitude; and He was moved with compassion for them, and healed their sick. [15]When it was evening, His disciples came to Him, saying, "This is a deserted place, and the hour is already late. Send the multitudes away, that they may go into the villages and buy themselves food."

[16]But Jesus said to them,
"They do not need to go away. You give them something to eat."

[17]And they said to Him,
"We have here only five loaves and two fish."

[18]He said, "Bring them here to Me." [19]Then He commanded the multitudes to sit down on the grass. And He took the five loaves and the two fish, and looking up to heaven, He blessed and broke and gave the loaves to the disciples; and the disciples gave to the multitudes. [20]So they all ate and were filled, and they took up twelve baskets full of the fragments that remained. [21]Now those who had eaten were about five thousand men, besides women and children.

CHAPTER ONE

"What do you want from us?"

"**W**HAT do you want from us? Do you want to convert us all? Do you want us to be your slaves forever?

"What do you want from us?"

If hatred had a face, it would have been his. Turban askew, eyes aflame, his mouth spewed the red-hot lava of "Jihad Jargon." Only the steel bars of the jailhouse window kept us from being consumed by this molten fury.

It was a terrible day in paradise. The gentle breezes of the Indian Ocean and Malacca Strait could not quench the fire. This Indonesian Imam would gladly have done Allah a favor and killed an American Christian. His rage resulted from a lifetime of serving Exxon/Mobil executives and sleeping in a one-room wooden coop while they danced the night away in high fashion. His people had waited hand and foot on the elite Dutch and Americans while the Java government collected the few crumbs falling from Aceh's tilted table. Finally he and the multitude he served had captured three of the oppressors and their Chinese friend, and justice would, if only for one torrid afternoon, be served.

USA Today said it was a group of missionaries who "ran to the police station for help when faced with the mob."

The Jakarta Morning Post said it was "another unfortunate incident of Moslem/Christian conflict." The world turned the page, drank their juice and coffee, and went on to discuss bigger things; but, for a group of people in Aceh, North Sumatra, the multitude was expressing its sense of injustice in what had become an international incident. March 1999 was just the tip of the iceberg of what would escalate into events that would polarize the world.

We had come to the town that morning in our desire to pray through Aceh. A day's journey north of the provincial border, the little town of Peralak is the last police post before a stretch of highway that has been a graveyard for police and freedom fighter alike. It is here that mass graves can be found. It is here that military do not travel at night. It is here that the seeds of rhetoric grow armies of youth ready to blow themselves up for the sake of the Militant Cause. Recruiting ground for extremists, it is here that children become adults before they shave and families send their young men to do Holy War against the infidels.

We arrived on a beautiful, calm, peaceful March morning looking forward to signing in at the checkpoint and going quickly on to Banda Aceh where there is some of the best scuba diving in the world. Our hired driver felt that he could make it very comfortably if we just had a bite to eat and got on the road again. Parking at a central area, we agreed that we would go through the market and on to the police station, register, and be on our way within an hour. We decided to go in two's so that we could see this quiet little town and share with each other what we had found.

A secondary school was dismissing for lunch and Friday prayers, and we were soon in the midst of hundreds of teenagers eager to try their English. Happy to oblige, we entered haltingly into conversation about the NBA and other American attractions important to youth. The young people were the same ages as our sons and daughters. It was fun to see how this half lived, what they thought about, what they studied, and what their sense of humor was. It was light fun and a real joy to be accepted by these young people. They noticed the books we had in the car and we were glad to give them a few. Finding that these books were written in their mother tongue of Acehnese, they became very interested. Soon 500 books and 90 cassette tapes in Acehnese were being handed about. It had taken about 45 minutes and parents were calling to young people to not be late for prayers.

In these villages, the Mosque is central to life. There is freedom of religion in Indonesia, but there is also civic pressure. The further from the capital one lives, the stronger the civic pressure. Their delay in reporting directly to the Mosque brought more than interest from the adults and, with apology, the students moved along quickly. They got to the Mosque at about the same time we got to the police station.

Our driver was at the station when we arrived. He worked for a company in another state and had registered his vehicle and shown the appropriate licenses. The police were professionally cordial and more than a bit interested in the books and tapes.

None of us read the language or spoke it. A friend had suggested we give these as gifts and so we seized the opportunity to have the officials translate for us the message we carried. A tape player was found and we began to listen together to the Christian message of the tape and soon realized that the book was the Gospel of Luke and the Book of the Acts of the Apostles from the Bible. Not illegal in Indonesia, these were not enough to set off any alarms with the police. They did caution us about the strong Islamic nature of the area where we were and suggested that we use some restraint in further contact. We assured them there was not a problem because the young people had exhausted our supply and we just wanted to pass through to the beautiful city several hours ahead.

We were invited into the police station so that our papers could be recorded and they could call to the station ahead to inform them of our departure time and a possible estimated time of arrival. The Indonesian police are very professional, thorough, and hospitable. We would soon also find out that they are even tempered, and very loyal to their guests. Hell was about to pour over from the Arab-looking building with the minaret.

We were in a comfortable room in the left rear of the police station. We had been offered cool drinks and made comfortable while a clerk recorded our passport and visa information. Calls were being made to be sure the way ahead was safe for us. We were really enjoying the good humor of our new found friends, more banter about Basketball and WWF and the recent Heavyweight Title Bout when conflict crashed against the windows.

"You mother _____! What do you want from us?" Not quite *Conversations in English Tape 3*, the language was sweet in light of the emotion in which it was hurled. A bottle accompanied it and broken glass flew through the room.

The police quickly pushed us into a hallway for cover and began to reprimand the man at the window. We checked each other for glass and, finding everyone alright, took up a safe place in a cell at the hallway's end. This would be our home for the next five hours as a multitude of very unhappy Moslems vented their hatred, anger, and frustration against fellow Moslems who happened to be doing their job in protecting a hapless group that was definitely in the wrong place at the wrong time. We were in the midst of a civil war with roots so deep no Westerner will ever understand.

With the man was a multitude and in response to our question, "What do they want?" the police officer replied, "You, dead."

Multitudes form when reason can no longer be found. They live in tent cities in the Sudan or gather on hill sides in Palestine. Multitudes lend their force of numbers to any cause. They can be mustered by high common fear or common need of common understanding. They gather in the desert in Arizona for Hedonism during the annual Burning Man Festival. They gather on the Mall in Washington for any number of causes. They gather at Tiananmen Square or Trafalgar Square or any square that can accommodate them. They march for causes, the environment, globalization, abortion rights, protest of political position, academic freedom, the need for food, money for AIDS.

Multitudes are harmless. They wait for trains, they escape heavy rains, and they attend sporting events. Multitudes walk through deserts to find water. They carry a few possessions on their backs to flee conflict. They are all in search of a few basic needs.

When a multitude forms and begins to move, leaders ask, "What do they want?"

With the multitudes of Cherokee who began to move west from the Appalachian Mountains, leadership said, "Do not worry; they will never survive the winter."

When multitudes were herded onto train cars to be destroyed under fascism it was said, "They are an inferior race; we do the world a favor to eliminate them."

When multitudes fled Atlanta in the face of Sherman's march to the sea, it was said, "Do not be afraid, the South shall rise again."

The problem with multitudes is they can be directed and affected by a very small group of very extreme people. Hatred grows in hungry bellies. Hatred spreads its ruinous roots until murder/suicide becomes a viable option to people hopelessly bound by the life sucking system. The multitude, once in motion, is an irresistible force about to meet government's immovable object. Once they swell the streets and get a taste of forbidden power, a multitude mutates into a mob that is viewed as a mutiny. Mutiny must be dealt with at all costs, so brother takes up arms against brother, nations align themselves against nations. And, people begin killing other people.

What every mass murderer needs is a multitude that will follow his direction. Whether they are disciplined and in uniform or undisciplined blowing themselves to bits makes little difference. They are a multitude. They want a slice of the pie, a crumb from the table, the freedom to farm, the right to have a child or gain an education.

The multitude is not mindless as some would think. The multitude come to the feet of the one they think can give them a better life. They commit to that way because they have a hope that these words will be different. They want to believe that their morsel will become a loaf if they just are willing to pay the price. And when it begins to appear that they have been used again, they turn their hopes to a better future for their children.

Would Aceh Province of North Sumatra, Indonesia, be any better off if it were governed by Islamic law? Would the rice grow taller? Would the fish return to the Straits of Malacca and be in abundance as they had been in times past? Would the passages of the straits be free from pirates? Would the money from Exxon/Mobil be shared in every home? This multitude, fueled by the rhetoric of a young man instructed in Arabia and armed by money from a man found in a hole in the earth believes with all its humble heart that the answer is an unequivocal "Yes."

Facing the first messenger of this multitude frightened

us to the core. There had been other multitudes, other countries, other causes, but the heat of this fire found fodder in our hearts. We could hear the multitude milling about the station. They threw rocks on the roof and bottles at the walls and windows. They chanted and cursed in English and Indonesian. They broke windows and cried out what they would do to us and to those who protected us.

The professional phrase is, "The situation has escalated." Across from me in the cell was the Banker, a three-time golden gloves champion of the State of New York. Black belt in several martial arts and no stranger to violent situations, he smiled. "Stay calm, this is a level 4, the police will just wait till they calm down. Stay away from the windows. Be still. Do not worry; the police know what to do."

I glanced at the Doctor, mild-mannered and a very close friend, he just smiled back. I am sure he was thinking of other situations we had been through. The veins on his forehead looked like they would burst at any moment.

The Asians were calm, poised. They have lived with Jihad for decades and know how to ride out the storm.

I decided to think through other multitude situations. Taking the Banker's advice, I sat down to quietly wait it out.

CHAPTER TWO

Multitudes are harmless

MULTITUDES are harmless. They gather where there is the hope of food, shelter, information or freedom. As long as no one ignites a fire in them, they can just go about their business with no sense of trouble. But, when a firebrand is let loose among them, they can quickly turn to a maelstrom of misery. Public safety is all about keeping the multitude from hurting themselves or others. A "Mad Man" manipulates the multitude to become a mob of anarchists bent on change at any cost and usually marching to the beat of his malfeasant melody.

"Sheep without a shepherd" is one description of a multitude. Among them you find the halt, the lame, and the blind, those too weak to sustain themselves. Within the multitude children are born and the elderly die. Moses' multitude moved at the pace of the slowest member. Few do. Most multitudes mill about as Israel did, taking 40 years to walk around in an area no bigger than an average Texas pasture.

When multitudes are united in the basic belief that they were born to their current estate and fated to remain in it, they settle down and suffer silently hoping for a brighter future in another life. "Well," they rationalize, "things could have been worse...I could have been a worm or some other hapless creature."

"Nepal is a Hindu nation," I was told in 1983. At the time I was under arrest for preaching Christianity. You see, Christianity is dangerous for those who control the multitude because it is all about a Carpenter who was a King, and a Lamb who was a Lion. In those contradictions is hope and hope is a dangerous thing. Hope will cause the multitude to rise up. The Romans found that Christianity would, if not contained by Public Security, "Turn the world upside down."

The multitudes of Nepal are today the focus of another group of "firebrands." Maoists, who must have missed the past 15 years of China's release of the multitudes, are trying to lead the irresistible multitude force against the immovable object of their King's believed divinity. The multitudes of Nepalese who just want to grow their rice in peace have become the most recent pawn in the hands of those who would like to own the Himalayas.

We had come there in 1983 at the request of a national Christian leader to tell them of a hope that they could not only have a better life, but would go to a better place when this life was over. This was a hope that could give them great joy in their family and as they toiled long hours in the rice paddy. We were perceived as firebrands by those in control of the multitude, but these detractors were also looking for an answer to their hopelessness.

Our days were spent trekking through some of the most beautiful villages on earth. The geographic plate carrying the multitudes of India has for centuries been in conflict with the continental plate carrying the multitudes of Chinese. This great collision of Homelands has given rise to the most majestic mountains on the planet. There among the up-thrust of time dwell a humble, hardworking multitude. Like all multitudes, they want something. Even as basic as life is for them, they would like to know who made the mountains and how all this came to be and who maintains it for them. They think that maybe the King of Nepal is connected to the gods and through him they have such beauty, they believe this because they had never had the opportunity to consider any other answer.

We came to them with something to be considered and they were very keen to hear. The plan had been to trek these mountains and distribute booklets in each place. The supply of literature at four levels of reading ability from cartoons to advanced vocabulary had been prepared in India and shipped by truck to Kathmandu. We flew there from several nations and, after five days of acclimatization were ready for the paths we would soon call "home."

The crates of literature looked like too many to distribute with our team of 40, but the zeal of the local man lifted us to new heights of belief. Whether to prove his point or not, he sent us to a village just outside Kathmandu for a little training exercise. We had a crate of small booklets that weighed more than 100 kilos and contained thousands of copies of a booklet entitled "Who is Jesus?".

Parking the vehicle at the center area of a village, we offloaded the cargo and prepared for an orderly distribution of the hope-filled material. Once the crate was open and the contents declared, the multitude's surge literally knocked us to the ground. They desperately wanted the printed material. Once they heard it was Christian, they could not be contained in their zeal to have it. They wanted the hope it contained.

We had to stand back to back and just throw it in the air. They took every page. They consumed it. Not one booklet was left on the ground. Not one page was torn. They came like ants to devour sugar. I had been amazed at the force of the multitude. We had not called to them. There had been no advance team telling them we would come on that day. It was mid-afternoon in a sleepy little village and suddenly a throng had appeared.

The multitude itself is harmless; but, when pointed toward hope, it becomes an irresistible force. The multitude in Aceh had been pointed toward a hope of independence from Jakarta. They had been preached a message of hope from the inequities of life. These Nepalese had heard of a book that would bring you hope and they were ready to go to any length to get a copy of that book. They were not being converted to a religion; they were being given a chance to have hope in their lives.

Will hope make your rice grow taller? Will hope make your children healthier? Will hope make your people more productive? The statistical answer is, "Yes." Studies by WHO, the UN, and Oxford University confirm a higher standard of living for cultures who have a sense of hope. The post-reform growth of China is little more than the fruit of giving Chinese the opportunity to hope again. The grandeur of their former culture was dashed to pieces in the hopelessness of the "cultural revolution." With hope restored, they have become world leaders in economic growth.

My arrest had come as the result of a multitude of schoolchildren opening our trekking baskets and taking out the booklets. We were on a break in a very remote place and these kids just helped themselves to our books. I had been amazed at their boldness, only to be assured by our local guide that it was not offensive in their culture and custom for someone to look through your bag to see what you were carrying. When they had seen it was books, they had decided to lighten our load.

They ran off giggling with delight at having "received" a book. We were observed by an official who felt it necessary to invoke Public Safety and so I was invited to explain myself to the local authority. He and I had a wonderful discussion about multitudes and the need to keep the people under control so that their safety could be insured. It made perfect sense to me and I assured him that I would do nothing that would cause unrest.

Then the most amazing thing happened, he asked for a copy of the book.

Was he joining the multitude? Was he really any different from the multitude? He had food. He had shelter. He had clothing. He had position. He had authority. He had education. He had a following. What was it that he did not have that would cause him to join the multitude?

He did not have the information his people had received. So, he would not be able to provide them public safety because they would be living at a level of understanding higher than his. His only hope to be able to continue to serve them would be to have the same level of information as they and that meant he had to arrest me to get a copy of the book that would give him hope. He wanted hope just like they wanted hope. You see, he was also a part of the multitudes.

It was that day that I learned to see all men as part of the multitude. We find that multitude of humanity in many different places. Some are in the valley of decision. How many people are there today who will not make some decision? Only those who are comatose will not make decisions. And, we don't know for sure how many decisions they will make. The multitudes that have to make decisions are going to follow the same path.

They will gather as much information as they can. They will wait as long as they can. They will interview or research others who have made the decision and evaluate the outcome to determine their decision. They will search their own hearts and read books of wisdom before making the decision. And, having done all this, when the situation allows no more delay, they will make a decision. And they will hope they had made the right decision.

Winston Churchill is quoted as having said, "There is no worse mistake in public leadership than to hold out false hopes soon to be swept away."

When America and Great Britain decided to go to war against Terrorism and that the battle ground would be Iraq, they gathered as much information as they could, waited as long as they could, sought history and other books, prayed, consulted with the multitudes under the tyranny of terror and said "OK, we will take this course of action, send the troops." And from the day they decided to make a strike against the cousins of Aceh, they had hoped they made the right decision. The justification for war has been, "To give hope to those who were under the tyrannical rule of Saddam Hussein."

Multitudes on both sides of the conflict are really looking for hope. Multitudes are harmless until someone points their frustrated futile feelings toward something called hope. And then they will cross seas, walk through deserts, chase mirages, deny themselves and pay any price to get hope.

The people who surrounded us in Nepal wanted a book that would give them hope. Because it was carried to them by Westerners who they perceived to be hopeful people, they were willing to receive that hope. The same villagers hide from the Maoists and have to be conscripted to military service because they see the Maoist cause as hopeless. If the King is in contact with the gods, then even if you kill his family, or have them killed, you will never have the hope of overthrowing him. And, why should we follow you if you haven't got a hope?

The multitude welcomed the Carpenter King to the city because they thought He would overthrow the Romans and they would get the tax money. He did not. Instead, the Romans captured Him and His followers and terrorized them for a night before beating and crucifying Him publicly so that they could bring that multitude back into proper order for their own safety.

However, that Lamb became the Lion when He rose from the dead and history records that within two months the multitude of His followers had grown past the previous high of 5,000 and was now beyond 10,000 and growing every day. The attempt to control the multitude had failed because they had found hope for their hopelessness in the One the grave could not contain.

The multitude is looking for hope. Whether they gather in stadiums or public lands, whether they walk the parched deserts or make small boats and risk all in shark-infested waters, they want hope. They want to believe that their leaders are telling them the truth. They are willing to die to provide hope for their children.

When I was arrested in Nepal, the penalty for changing religion was one year in jail. The penalty for leading someone to pray to change religion was three years per person. The penalty of identification with Hope in Christ through water baptism was six years in jail. The multitude was willing to take the risk.

Why? They had heard about hope and were willing to give all to have it. The police went through the village to re-collect the materials. Of 100 kilos of booklets, thousands of pieces of paper, only five were surrendered as evidence. Even the man in charge did not surrender his copy to add to the pile; instead, he quietly slipped it into his jacket pocket, a piece of hope to be secured toward a better day.

***

While the Militant Moslem Multitude circled our public security sanctuary, I thought of the power of the printed page to propel the multitude to hope. Hope will never make you ashamed. Hope will carry you through death. Suddenly I was aware that all this thought of hope was becoming an anchor to my emotions. Looking at the others in our group I could see in their eyes that same hope. There was no fear, just a certain expectation that the One who had led us to this place would be the One who would take us out of it, either to this life or to another.

The multitude became impatient and tried to rush the facility only to be driven back by a volley of rubber bullets and tear gas. Their impatience told us that the false hope of whatever had been told them by the Irate Imam was beginning to wear off. They would need another dose of rhetoric before they would again rush the building. The wait gave me time to reflect on another multitude I had seen.

The human sea lay still before us

THE human sea lay still before us. Morning light and
the gentle breeze started the swells that would become
waves so great in size that any tardy tourist would be swept
up in their undertow. Multitudes of men and women sought
serene seconds on the rocky shore of the Beijing Train
Platform.

The smell of unwashed human flesh melded with city
stench to say to all, "It is another day of overpopulation."
Steam engines, coal burners, 50 seats for 200 people,
uniforms demanding identification, hopes and dreams of
seeing long-lost loved ones dashed as conductors drove
them from the train. It was China before the reforms and it
was a multitude desperately seeking some hope.

At one time they had been the most advanced culture
on earth. Five thousand years of written history had been
replaced by "simple characters" or illiterate masses. Hope
that had built the Great Wall and the Grand Canal had been
replaced by communist corruption that made the Confucian
code little more than a pile of stones kept in Xian with all
the other relics of a long-gone past. We stood that morning
observing a multitude in misery.

1985 was one of those years tucked in the confusion of the post-Mao era. It had been 11 years since the death of the Great Hope of the people. Eleven years of hopelessness created by the dilemma between "giving him face" and "saying he was wrong." All the positions of leadership were in the hands of those who had marched with Mao. The people wore the blue tunic and trousers of the peasant while the leaders tried to fit their extended bellies into the green of the military. One in every five of the one billion people was in some way connected to those whose charge it was to preserve "public security."

Hope had been broken down to: "I hope the cadre decides to have us eat today." Work units traveled in sweat-box train cars or marched from task to task. Human value had been eradicated from the society. The mindless multitudes of the Cultural Revolution had settled the matter of hope 20 years before when, as children, these before us had seen the consequence of hope's expression. There was to be no individual expression that might release hope in the population. Anyone expressing free thought was a counter revolutionary and would die before hope could be engendered.

Hundreds of dramas were created to depict Mao as a god, the great deliverer of the masses. The Book of Hope was burned in great rallies and anyone found holding it would be beaten and imprisoned. In its place were the jumbled verses of the Great Chairman, the Liberator of the Masses. His *Little Red Book* became the standard for thought and, small as it was, so was its content.

A pingpong ball gave hope to the person serving it. Launched from a Chinese paddle, it created a rhythmic hope of return, of victory, of individual triumph over challenge, of a name rather than a number. When the two great powers came together it was the little bouncing ball that paved the way to our standing at dawn on the worn cobblestones of the Beijing Central Train Station. Time had slowly claimed each of the hopeless neo-mandarin magnates and it was the dawning of a new day for China.

Hope produces patience. We will wait for what we hope for. Just three miles from where we stood, a younger political leader who had not been in the Long March faced the morning with hope in his heart. He saw a new China. He saw a productive people released from State-run unproductive dungeons of despair to a hope of ownership and enterprise. He held in his heart the hope that one day China would lead the world. He saw a China in which the people would no longer sleep in the filth of the street guarded by green suits on the soil of their own land. Hope kept him while the system wound down to a handful of those who had made the Long March.

Deng Xiao Ping would one day lead this multitude to hope. He would bring the reforms so very essential. They would craft a future for their children and their children's children. Music would ascend from parks and playgrounds and nations would again gather for great banquets. Space would be explored and medical research allowed. The pingpong ball would become a basketball and one day, the Olympic Games would bring all the nations to see what Mao could not, a China by, of, and for the Chinese.

Between his residence and the train station was the tomb of Chairman Mao and the cobblestones of Tiananmen Square. The blood of one had seized the multitude in the grip of false hope. A system from France, Western philosophy, had swept toward the sunrise in post-war Europe and Asia. A great alliance of false hope had marched multitudes to unproductive bondage. Lenin had learned, Marx and Engle had left their hope-filled Judaism hoping to find identification with the masses. Ho Chi Minh had traveled to France to appeal for freedom for his people only to find the same false hope. Europe's reaction to the first war was to foster a false dream in which all would be equal without recognizing the love and hope of God. And, in the spiritual vacuum left by Marx, leaders became divine. The little embalmed man in the square had become god to the multitudes and, with his death, there was nothing left to give hope.

There would be blood shed on those cobblestones. We could feel the tension as we traveled in 1985. The young people (radiant in the hope that youth holds until it is smashed from them) would never sustain the empty ideology that kept them from education and the arts. They were Chinese. In their blood were the great engineers and architects, the great painters and poets, the great philosophers, the world's first linguists. They could never remain mindless multitudes in the hands of a few. This morning they slept on cobblestones under cardboard, but a day would come when they would be free from bondage, educated, and connected to the nations about which they had heard.

His dark eyes arrested my thoughts as he softly said, "Hello." It was a voice, a sound recognizable from the faceless sea. A nation, a people called out in that one voice. I looked at him and saw the hope in his eyes.

"Hello," I responded. "How are you?"

"Fine, thank you. And you?" Conversation…we were having a conversation. The sea became people; and people, a person with a name and a mind and a future and a hope.

The sound of the metal taps on issued boots broke it up. He buried his face and I turned to greet the five green shirts that came to make sure public safety was maintained. After all, if this fellow got a bit of hope, he might run amuck and arouse the multitude and the wave might just break in the wrong, uncontrollable direction of the Great Hall of the People.

They herded us through the sea. Arms and legs moved at the sound of their boots. We were very well protected from thieves, and anyone else who might want to come in contact. Herded to the Foreigners Waiting Area we sat in overstuffed chairs under Humphrey Bogart fans and pondered the plight of the cobblestone crowd. From no window could they be seen. Their voices could not reach through the heavy wooden doors and they most certainly would never be allowed to use the toilet or the hot water cascading from a long-forgotten spigot. I tried to stem the flow but to no avail. It would have taken hope for future hand-washings for someone to actually replace the corroded stopcock. I suppose under Mao they learned that the hot water would never end for the privileged.

Placed in the watchful care of the Waiting Room Matron, we sipped tepid tea and thought about our journey to Siberia. We were going to go across Europe reaching London in time to fly back to the States. We had come up from Hong Kong with a couple of backpacks of Bibles, the only book of true hope. Having delivered them in Beijing, we now had materials for the anticommunist multitude who had ridden the rails in reverse. Herded onto cars, they had left their beautiful cities and winding streams to be reeducated in the mindless wastes of Siberia. With art and science in their genes, they had been separated from the multitudes.

Stalin had said that he would, "Wipe out Christianity in one generation." These youth had been born to Christian parents in Siberia and were very strong in their faith. They had hope that one day people would ride the rails and bring them the book that would give hope. As we thought through the days we would face, one thought kept creeping into our conversation.

"Would we see that young person again?"

Sure, he would be in the face of the emerging generation around the world. But, we wanted to see him, the person. We decided that, once on board the train, we would walk through every car in the hope of seeing him. Statistically, there was a very slim chance of it happening, but hope is never the captive of statistics. With hope we waited for the Matron to lead us to the conductor who would accompany us to our places and instruct those around us not to, "bother them with questions or try to talk with them."

The hopeless that herd the masses have lost all sense of the practical or real. Entrapped in their obsession to prevent hope, they really believe that 60 people in a train car with four Westerners who are obviously open to dialogue are going to ride for three days and not say "hello." As soon as the train left the station the bilingual dictionaries came out, the family photos followed, and we were introduced to a wonderful international group set on the hope of arriving at their destinations with some contact or friend from outside the mindless mob.

But, the comfort of the foreign cabin was not the beach upon which the tide of Chinese humanity rested. It was, we found, in another section of the train, at the rear. Off we went to find our "happy-faced youth."

There are a lot of Chinese people. When you start looking through them for one face, it really is like looking for a needle in a haystack. But, each face is unique. No two Asians look exactly alike and we knew we could find our man if we just looked into the three or four hundred faces on that train.

Once clear of the city, the steam locomotive strained in the hope of reaching the summit of Badaling before plunging into the Mongolian Desert. Chinese people like to smoke and spit. The space between cars is a perfect place for both. It has a breeze, you can spit all you want and no one will tell you to stop smoking. As the train lurched along at high speed, these couplings are an adventure in humanity. Passing through the one between car 17 and 18 I saw our man.

Face washed, hair combed, travel shirt neat, but he was definitely the one I had seen. I stood in a space vacated by a smoker/spitter and waited to see if this young man would reach across the great wall of hopelessness to again make contact.

"Good morning." He smiled as I recognized the sound of his voice.

My hope fulfilled, I returned the greeting and then released a torrent of very high-speed English. His puzzled face put the brakes on my runaway zeal. It is true; hope fulfilled will energize individuals in the multitude to a reckless rampage.

"How are you?" I asked.

"Fine, thank you. How are you?" We were in *Conversations in English Tape 1* for sure.

"What is your name?" I asked.

"Wang Shu Ming," he answered, and then quickly regained the proper side of the conversation, "Where do you come from?"

"America." The answer brought hope to his eyes.

"Where are you going?" he asked, and I could see the pages in the book turning.

"I am going to Harbin, where are you going?" Harbin was a near destination and kept us in China.

"I also am going to Harbin." His smile was so broad. We had made a connection, a similarity that would be the first stone in a bridge of relationship. The pingpong ball had crossed the net and we both were experiencing hope.

"Do you live in Harbin?" I asked.

"No." He struggled with the vocabulary necessary for a more complete answer.

We were joined in the passage by four or five others who leaned close to hear the words. They were so very curious about English and who we were and what we were doing. Little did we know the risk he was taking by talking to "foreigners."

"I a student." It would take years for me to learn that in Chinese the context reveals verb tense. He had struggled through a most difficult exercise; trying to remember the "verb to be" and to express it properly. He had given up the struggle rather than lose the opportunity. He was hoping this time could develop into brighter things.

"These are students also?" I asked, looking around at the eavesdroppers.

Ignoring my questions he looked out the smoke-stained window and shuffled his feet. "See you again," he said, as he headed back to the hard-seat section designated for him.

"Ok," I said. Losing hope I turned to go back to my section, 14 cars forward. It was then I saw the green shirt in the window. Contact with foreigners was discouraged as it could affect public security.

Coming from a free and outspoken America, we often do not understand the pressures of the multitudes held by hopeless ideology. The youth in Aceh had made contact with us which threatened those who herded them through life. They would learn Arabic instead of English. This would guarantee that they would never read medicine or other advanced education tracks. However, their ruling class would send their children to Harvard or Oxford or Sydney so that a representative contact could be made with the outside world. Reforms would be very slow in coming to the masses. For many more years in China, a young person who found a way to learn English would be the suspect of a mindless green shirt whose only task was to keep the herd moving in the prescribed circuits of life — far enough from the horizon to never allow hope to be seen.

That night he risked it all. We would arrive in Harbin in the morning and he wanted desperately to hope for the future so while the green shirts slept he made his way to the foreigner car. With the stealth of a night cat he sought me out.

"What is your name?" He asked excitedly.

"My name is Mark." I answered leaving complete control to him.

"Are you a Christian?" I was shocked at the question.

"Yes," I answered.

"Have you any 'bread?'" He was asking about Bibles.

"Yes," I answered. "I have five 'whole loaves.'"

"May I have them?" His hope-filled voice touched a fountain of emotion in my heart.

"Of course," I responded. "Here they are."

"Goodbye." It was final and yet eternal. Two words that have warmed my soul ever since.

How had he known? Was the cobblestone welcome a chance meeting? Had someone told him we would be on that train? In those days you never knew who knew you. We had to be so very careful with everything. Any wrong word could mean jail for many people. Now, with Bibles printed and purchased openly in China, with churches open and packed for every service, I often wonder if hope was fulfilled through those young ones who rode the rails.

✻✻✻

My thoughts were interrupted by another crashing bottle and the sound of gunfire. This was a really tense situation. I looked at the Banker and he held up five fingers. Not tight yet. How long would it be before these young people would know the hope that drove my young Chinese friend to find me on a moving night train? Would they find it? Would they ever be free of the hatred and killing? Would the Irate Imam control their lives forever?

CHAPTER FOUR

The multitude has many faces

THE multitude has many faces. It is a mosaic of colors and shapes. No eye in a multitude looks exactly like any other eye. When massed together and motivated in a direction, they become an irresistible force that is headed for an immovable object. When I was asked to visit Jakarta, Indonesia, during the student demonstrations leading up to the fall of the Suharto regime, I wondered at the wisdom of a Westerner being anywhere near the place.

Local leaders with whom I had spent days in prayer felt that the young people were becoming pawns in the hands of masters who would use them to cause civil war in their country. It was the end of the school term and the very least that could be said was that their education was going to be interrupted. Remembering Kent State and our own campus demonstrations, I agreed to meet them in Jakarta.

Indonesia is a beautiful place. The 15,000 islands are a string of magnificent pearls strung through crystal-clear waters with sandy beaches and majestic volcanoes; it is a sight to behold. From the beginning of time it has been the habitation of nations speaking their own languages, embracing their own cultures, fashioning their own gods, preserving their own hopes and dreams.

In the post-world-war era, someone decided that unity among the peoples was the way of providing a future hope for generations to come, and since the Dutch had colonized the islands in the first place, they were the logical stewards of the riches that they would surely develop for the benefit of the multitudes. The only difficulty in that stewardship was there were several other groups who claimed the right to give hope. The Indians had been there first. Then had come the Chinese who, about 600 years ago, had made a slick cohabitation deal with the Indians where the Chinese stayed out of government and just made money.

About 1305, the first Moslems came to Aceh and then throughout the western islands. They too were tradesmen. The cultures coexisted quite well as long as they did not try to unify the languages, education, and currency. Even the Dutch were sensitive to the fact that the 10,000 distinct ethnic groups of Indonesia had no desire to intermarry, unify economically, or exchange gods.

Then the modern era came. With the Japanese gone, Indonesia was given back to the Dutch. The Indonesians did not like the Dutch and a very bloody war ensued as the multitude united in a common purpose to rid themselves of the Dutch. This was not at all difficult because, in post-war Europe, the Dutch were not all that strong anyway.

The multitude was unified under the leadership of President Sukarno and the famous teacher Hatta. The Sukarno-Hatta regime continued along a bumpy path until recently, with the daughter of Sukarno, Mrs. Megawati Sukarno Putri, sitting on the throne over the multitude which is now 200-million strong.

The nation is now estimated to be 90% Moslem, making it the largest Moslem nation in the world.

The multitude continues to teem about looking for hope.

The Indonesian political process is motorized mayhem. Youth, the life of multitudes, is paid to cavort about the streets in truckloads and on motorbikes declaring their loyalty to the candidates of the various parties. One week is green week, so they wear the green shirts and chant the green chants and make a lot of noise about the green candidates. The following week is "red" week. So the same youth get paid to put on the red shirts and ride about in trucks and on motorbikes and proclaim to anyone who will listen the conquering virtues of the "red" candidate. The following week is the "gold" week and so the same youth put on the gold shirts and ride about in trucks and on motorbikes and proclaim the virtues of the "gold" candidate.

As one Singaporean observer put it, "This would never happen in Singapore."

There are two major problems with this system. It tends to undermine any hope of a peaceful and sincere election. And, intimidation by mindless mobs is dehumanizing at best. One day, three young men with green headbands and T-shirts drove up on the sidewalk to shout in my face the virtues of their candidate while revving the motor so loud it was impossible to discern anything they were saying.

The subliminal message was very clear, "This is our time to feel power and control. It is the only time we have, so we are enjoying it."

People without hope will always grab at the straws intimidation holds out to them. I have often wondered if any of those kids had been recruited and trained for the ultimate power trip, push this button and you enter paradise and do Allah a favor by killing the infidels. They are cute on the bikes with their T-shirts, but they would certainly look different holding a sword over the head of a hapless truck driver who had hoped to feed his family.

"We really need to pray," my friends said. "These elections are different. Mobs have begun burning our buildings, pastors are being killed, and we feel that students are going to be dragged into it." Indonesians all, they really love their country and, as part of the Christian Minority, they feel their only answer is prayer. They do not want to rule. They have no interest in any kind of takeover. They just do not want the heated rhetoric of a political false hope to ignite fires of hatred that cannot be quenched. Indonesia has released the multitude to determine their own course and there are people who will try to lead it to the removal of those who disagree with their ideology.

For this pre-election trip, we chose a five-star hotel for our "prayer tower." From our window we could see the formations of soldiers and police sent to defend the national congress building. We took turns praying through the night. We were impartial in our devotion, simply asking God to protect this multitude. They were dispersed in their representative colors and, from that pristine perch, they looked for all the world like sheep without a shepherd. With dawn came the stirring of hearts that would bring us to one of the most interesting multitude situations I have ever seen.

"Last time they gathered at the Sukarno-Hatta monument to begin their march," my host offered. "Let's go over there and see if that is the plan today." He checked us out of the hotel saying that we would be safer at his place outside Jakarta for the evening. He was torn between our mission and our safety, trying to find in his soul an island in the multitude big enough to accommodate hope for both.

"Do you think we could stay here another night?" I asked. Even with a one-night stay I was suffering separation anxiety.

"No, Mark," was his gentle reply. "Friends we have

in the government feel that this area could be a war zone by evening. You will come out and stay with us. We do not want to lose you to an angry mob."

"What does he know that I don't?" I wondered as we waited for the driver to bring his car.

The driver dropped us at the memorial and left to take our bags to the place where we would be staying. We were joined by some church members and took some time to pray for Indonesia. The hope that these men and women held in their hearts had unified education and given many human rights to Indonesia. They had created a government that could be for and by the people, but their hopes for wealth had corrupted their supposed ideals. They had become the "New Dutch" alien to the multitude; they had skimmed 20% of the economy into their family pockets. The demonstrations we would see this day were the corporate complaint of a multitude that had followed a false hope. They would wear different colors, shout different slogans, carry different placards, but their cry was the same, "You told me to hope in you and you didn't produce!"

Shifting location to the main university we found a sea of students pouring out into the streets. No hasty exodus from exams, this was a very well-planned public protest against the government in power. The multitude wanted change. The speeches were well prepared and delivered. My host was moved to tears many times and, as a friend, I tried to feel what he was feeling. It is not my country. I love Indonesia, but I could not make the bridge to the depth of his emotion. This giant of a man stood and wept as the future of his nation cried out their hope.

They began to move. Slowly, calmly, boundaries secured by students linked arm in arm, they moved through the streets and thoroughfares of Jakarta. Size makes a statement, but self control makes a declaration. These were very self-contained. They checked everyone who wished to join them. They wanted to be certain that none of the instruments of violence so common to Indonesian demonstrations was present. They were not against anything; they were for the future of their nation. I was proud to walk with them and to think of the future that could be realized if ever the interest groups would just allow these young people to emerge.

I lost my sense of direction. Usually, if I have walked a city I am pretty secure in my memory of it. I had become enthralled with the hope of these young people. After hours of flowing with them I realized I had no idea where I was. My friend seemed peaceful, but I began to get the sense of some coming difficulty and then, rounding a bend in the road, I saw it.

We had come full circle through the city and were approaching the congress building. The driver appeared and we left the crowd for the sanctuary of his car. He took us to a place near the hotel and we got down. Now, behind the military position, we sought a place for prayer. As we crossed through a parking garage near the congress we were greeted by companies of troops. Just getting ready for action, they were formidable.

"Mark," my friend called me. "How close do you want to get. This looks pretty serious."

"Let's see how far we can go before they stop us," I responded, realizing they would defend public safety.

We quickly moved up a walled walkway which deposited us to the right of the carpark of the congress. From there we could walk through the lines of police until we came to the commandos and the marines. There, about 500 meters ahead of us were the students. They had stopped in the street and were listening to speeches. We were in the midst of the military deployment in the south-bound side of the highway. All traffic had been rerouted to the north-bound lane. Its five lanes had no hope of containing the vehicles and a new multitude of youth approached from behind our position. They were not the docile student types.

These wore headbands and carried sticks and other home-fashioned weapons. It was not clear if they had come to "help" the police or if they had another agenda. We could feel the squeeze and prayed as the captain went over to negotiate with their leadership. Quite vocal and gesturing their dislike for the government and disdain for authority, this multitude threatened to turn an interesting study in democracy into a blood bath.

"These are the ones you have to watch," my friend said. "Sometimes they are paid by the government to start trouble so that the troops can rush in and 'restore order.' Watch about five rows back and see if they have weapons."

The Marine standing next to us said, "Where do you come from?"

"Wow," I thought. "Polite conversation in the midst of strife, now this is a man who knows the situation."

"I'm from America," I answered. "Have you been there?"

"Yes," he responded. "We were there last year to train with the US Marines."

"Did you enjoy it?" I asked.

"Of course, it is the most powerful country in the world and a very nice place to be."

"Thank you." I felt better having a friend in the Marines. His eyes never left the field in front of us as he spoke.

"Do you understand what is going on here?" he asked. "This is all about power. Today, we have it. The students will have it when they finish school. The gang across the way has no power. They never will because they do not have the discipline necessary to have power in their lives."

"Thank you for that explanation. What do you think is the source for all power?" Why not try to follow through with this young man?

"Well, everyone has to believe in something that will take care of him. You can believe in God, yourself, your captain, your Imam; but, you have to believe in something or someone." I was startled by the matter-of-fact way in which he presented his thoughts. This was not a mindless marine who could not make it. This young man was about the same age as those in the other groups. I wondered what a good thinker like him was doing out here.

"So you chose the military route?"

"Yes, Sir," he responded. "At the end of the day the military has the power in our country. When these two groups have had their say, we will still be standing."

Our conversation was interrupted as he came to alert position. The group of students had begun to move toward us. The group on our left had stopped behind the highway barrier. They were beginning to lose hope in their conquest. My new friend was tuned to his commander and I was in the way. I moved out of the formation and, standing on the side, prayed for all to be safe.

Two multitudes, one in uniform and one in Levis and T-shirts, faced each other over a slowly diminishing space of five-lane paved highway. The pressure grew with every step. Rumor had it that the students would rush the police and military to take and hold the congress, making a televised address to the nation. They had, evidently, never talked with this young marine. He was sure it would never happen.

They closed the gap to 200 meters and stopped. The marines had not lifted a voice or weapon. They just stood there as the immovable object.

A group of about 50 students came forward to within 100 meters and began to sing and chant slogans and dance.

It was very expressive, but lost on the marines. They were joined by a slight, well-dressed woman and a man with a stepladder and camera. I was amazed as my host explained to me that it was Maria Resa from CNN. She was going to make a report on the demonstration from right there.

She interviewed the group and they sang and waved banners and she thanked them and left. It was the most amazing bit of news reporting I had ever seen. I later viewed the report and you would have thought that every student in Indonesia was dancing 100 meters from congress.

After she left, the small group returned to the large one and together they began to advance on the marine position. When they came to the 100-meter position, the marines came to the full ready and their officer stepped forward about 20 meters and announced to the students that their demonstration had come as far as they would be allowed to come.

Two of the students stepped out to meet him and shouted some rather discourteous remarks to him and the multitude behind him. They stood their ground, but the students began to again move forward.

I called to my new marine friend, "Want to see some real power?" And, extending my hands to heaven, I cried out, "Lord, make these kids sit down."

They did. They sat right down. If there had not been a couple hundred military witnesses there I would believe this story to be untrue. The situation looked hopeless, but there is always hope in prayer. Those young people sat down in the street, contemplated their futures, and, in the calm declaration of their quality, quietly got up and dispersed.

The multitude has a face. It is made up of many faces. Each one is unique. When the Indonesian is under pressure, he is all smiles. The students were smiling. The Marines were smiling. The commander was smiling. The situation was a controlled expression of the desire for hope.

When an Indonesian stops smiling, the lava of a thousand volcanoes cannot compare to the fury that is about to spill out. Centuries of repression at the hands of foreign invaders and charm-wielding spiritists give flame to the timeless passions of these tribal, territorial, traditional inhabitants of the land. In recent years some have reverted to cannibalism as Dayak repelled Madurese in the conquests of cultures gone mad. Acehnese and Javanese fill mass graves in Sumatran paradise; and, into the tropical tapestries of Timor and Ambon are woven the scarlet threads of the blood of their sons.

From the sounds outside our cell, no one was smiling. We were about to have a visitor. The multitude was about to have a face, and what a face it would be. Not the Irate Imam, not the youth so hungry for hope, this would be the face of authority.

CHAPTER FIVE

Ten men turned the corner

TEN men turned the corner and walked toward us. Known to each other, they carried the weight of an escalating situation. The five in uniform walked with the confident stride of men trained for such a circumstance. Those in civilian dress were showing the strain of throwing back the first organized attack by this group of radicals. I was relieved that the Irate Imam was not with them for I thought he would get physical if we were brought face to face.

The Captain of Police was the first to speak. He gave us an overview of the situation. We had arrived at the wrong place, at the wrong time, and had done the wrong thing. The Moslem population was very upset about the books and tapes, but that was not the main situation. They saw us as intruders into holy territory and felt compelled to cleanse the land. That would mean our removal. He had arranged for our car to be allowed to pass through them. We were to wait just a few minutes and then follow him and the five uniforms to the car, get in, and get out of town headed back to where we had come from and definitely to never return. He had negotiated this solution.

From behind his well-apportioned frame stepped a man about my age who had pulled an "I Love America" T-shirt over the top of his rotund physique. The effect made the Eagle appear wall-eyed. Trying not to laugh with relief at the comedy before me, I bit the inside of my lower lip and focused on his sweating brow which was about a foot in front of my own.

"You are so stupid!" I'm not sure which hit me first, the fire of his passion or the spit that accompanied the insult from his lips. Now here was a man who had waited a long time to get an American in a compromised situation and tell him exactly how he felt about things. I wonder how many times an employer, teacher, or boss had said those words to him. They had lain in the bottom of this volcano for a long time.

"What have you done?" He was trying to make a point, but his body was trembling with such passion that his mind was receiving the verbal missiles in an erratic staccato which flew from his lips. His eyes, fixed on mine, were actually trembling in their sockets. The fire of his fury emblazoned his brow and his veins were like the tentacles of a giant squid, reaching to his temples. I have never seen a more angry man.

"Why have you come here?" Fury does not want an answer to such rapid-fire questions, but fearing for his health, I answered.

"Sir," I tried to step back a bit but was against a wall. "I am very sorry for the problem we have caused here. Please forgive us and allow us to go. We will bother you no more."

With a grunt he continued, closing whatever space I had managed to gain.

"You are fools. We have peace here. We are all one nation. I am a Moslem, this man is a Christian. We are good friends and neighbors. We have known each other since we were small and have grown up together. Our children are friends. This is not Ambon. We have peace here." He had used apology-purchased time to put together his entire instruction. He was beginning to calm and had diverted attention to his "friend."

The latter face was a classic of a person who had been grabbed by someone else who had an idea. He no more wanted to be there than did we. He was speechless. A "Christian" with four other Christians and he had nothing to say in any language. I looked at him with great love. If he were a Christian, then he would have gained hope from the fact that he was not forgotten by his brothers who live with real freedom. If he were not a Christian, then his ruse would not go unnoticed in heaven.

Nodding toward him, I tried to see some recognition of hope in his eyes. There was none that I could see. The only distinguishing characteristic I could see was the hat he wore.

Indonesia is the land of the "losers." Before the championships of the major American sports, T-shirts and ball caps are made declaring each team to be the winner and therefore Champion. Hundreds of thousands of these shirts and caps are made so that in the frenzy of victory fans will spend ridiculous amounts to have the "authentic championship shirt or cap."

Obviously, someone wins, and someone loses. Indonesia gets all the loser hats. They declare the championship of the ones who lost the game. I suppose Indonesia is far enough away from America that no one really knows or cares who won.

This "brother" was wearing a New York cap that would have fit a person about two-thirds his size. Perched on the top of a very round head, it said, "I am very uncomfortable with this situation and have no idea why I am in this place. They just grabbed me and stuck this stupid hat on my head and told me not to talk. Please do not prolong this because I want to get out of here."

Seeing the fear in his eyes, I said again we were sorry and looked beyond the now still volcano to the Police Officer.

They took their leave and we prepared to follow.

"We will come and get you," the officer said. "There is a large crowd outside, they may shout at you and throw things. Please stay with my men and get quickly into the car. We will hold them off."

He then said something to the Indonesian driver, checked to see that the hat and T-shirt had cleared the area and led us to the front of the station. We quickly began to get into the car, but the mob rushed across the highway and, throwing rocks, bottles, and insults, tried to capture their trophy Americans. We retreated into the building, but noticed the driver had blended with the crowd and disappeared.

It wasn't long before the smoke told the story. Our car was being burned. Wondering about the things in it, and happy the police had our passports, we reassembled ourselves in the cell and assessed the situation. Strain was on our faces, but calm was in our hearts. We had an assurance that it would all work out.

The officer returned to ask us to stay away from the windows. He was very upset. It was while he spoke to us that the electric power was cut off. He looked at us with consternation, turned on his heel, and took command of the situation. He too had become the object of the fury of this multitude.

"These Signs Shall Follow"

Mark 16:15-18

[15]And He said to them, "Go into all the world and preach the gospel to every creature. [16]He who believes and is baptized will be saved; but he who does not believe will be condemned. [17]And these signs will follow those who believe: In My name they will cast out demons; they will speak with new tongues; [18]they will take up serpents; and if they drink anything deadly, it will by no means hurt them; they will lay hands on the sick, and they will recover."

Acts 2:40-45

[40]And with many other words he testified and exhorted them, saying, "Be saved from this perverse generation." [41]Then those who gladly received his word were baptized; and that day about three thousand souls were added to them. [42]And they continued steadfastly in the apostles' doctrine and fellowship, in the breaking of bread, and in prayers. [43]Then fear came upon every soul, and many wonders and signs were done through the apostles. [44]Now all who believed were together, and had all things in common, [45]and sold their possessions and goods, and divided them among all, as anyone had need.

CHAPTER SIX

Multitudes want hope

MULTITUDES want hope. Believers in a cause think they have hope so they take action. They are all about action.

"What do you do?" This is their favorite question. They have developed from the idealism of the students sitting in the Jakarta Street, to the action figures that ride the bikes and shout the slogans. "What you think" has become "What you do" in the mind of a believer.

The ones getting the press today believe in a god who would direct you to hijack a plane full of innocent people and fly it into a building of innocent people to protest the way you were treated when you were a highly-paid US operative in a war between Afghanistan and Russia. That's a stretch, but if enough of the multitude can be persuaded to believe it, then believers they will become and airports around the world will ask you to remove your belt and shoes before you board an aircraft.

One believer, totally convinced, can change the course of human history.

Ivana Madzur is such a person. It was 1985, there was still a wall in Berlin and the Russians were occupying

Ivana's native Poland. Our group had crossed Siberia from China and we were hungry. We stayed at Szymanski's house near the Warsaw train station and had taken advantage of a beautiful spring morning to tour the Old City of Warsaw. Being a fan of Leon Uris, I had deeply wanted to see the ghetto from which a band of young Jews had the belief that they could overthrow Hitler and the Warsaw Uprising had occurred.

In the north-west corner of the Old City Square there is a sewer grate. It probably doesn't mean much to many; but reading Uris, it had come alive to me. It was through this grate that curriers entered a maze of pipe that carried their preteen bodies to leaders of the resistance. Their courage will never be forgotten. They had stepped out from the multitudes acquiescing to Hitler's maniacal systematic destruction of their city, their world, their hope.

To the right, in front of the grate, is a museum of the underground. I could have stayed on its second floor for a year. Sights and sounds I had tried to imagine while reading the printed page by flashlight hidden under blankets lest my parents would enforce their "get to bed" edicts, came to life as I stood in that place. A group of youth who decided that they would rather die believing than live without hope had created a legacy that inspired their neighbors to organize and, until they were sold out to Stalin, resist that tyranny to their death.

Hunger and the smell of pizza enticed me from study. One of our team had to eat every six hours and he had found a pizza place. We stepped reverently across the grate and entered a wonderful place. The sights and sounds were just like the home we had left a month before. The people looked like Americans. The cheese smelled like America. The tables and chairs felt like America and we could even hear a young guide sharing information with her English charge. Relaxed with hot pizza we began to laugh about many of the adventures we had faced on the Trans-Siberian Railway. Our team was made of believers who took Jesus literally when He said, "Go into all the earth and preach the gospel to every creature..."

Overheard in the small shop, we were surprised when the young lady asked us if we were Christians. Evidently we had let down our guard in the familiar surroundings. She invited us to a meeting that night at a Catholic Charismatic fellowship outside Warsaw. Intrigued, we agreed to go and arrangements were made.

We met with a group of about 20 students. They sang, accompanied by a guitar, and raised their hands in praise in charismatic fashion. We shared some of our stories of the journey and brought them a report of the church in China and Mongolia and the contacts we had made in Siberia and Moscow. Believers under the oppression of Communist Moscow, they were thrilled to hear of the believers on campuses across the railway. Of particular interest were the fellowships we had found in Irkutsk and Novosibirsk. We spent a wonderful evening and returned to the city filled with wonder at the faithfulness of the Lord.

I met and worked with Ivana many times after that. Through a series of events I was invited to spend three weeks in Poland traveling to universities and sharing my belief with students. At one time I was invited to join a Bishop in a public communion for solidarity and I was privileged to meet with many of the leaders of the Solidarity movement which eventually toppled Soviet power and saw the return of Poland to the Poles. But my experiences in that wonderful land paled in comparison to her testimony.

Ivana is a believer. Belief activates hope to performance. Signs follow those who believe. Nations are changed by those who believe. Jesus said of those who believe in Him that they would relieve the oppressed, they would bring healing, and they would be able to communicate with many nations. Ivana is a believer.

It was on my third visit that a colleague of hers told me the story. Ivana was too modest to tell it herself. As a schoolgirl she had profound faith in Jesus Christ. She believed with all of her little being that Jesus could keep her in the face of whatever oppression came up. She was never afraid to pray for a friend or give a loving hand when there was a need. She believed in her Bible and carried it in her book bag.

They were poor people in a poor country. All the material goods they produced rode the rails back to Mother Russia. The men and women of their villages worked long hours for little wage and the proceeds were sent to Moscow to fuel the arms race.

The students attended a rural school which was heated by a single coal-burning stove in the center of the room. Their punishment for any happy behavior was to go to the coal bin under the building and hand-carry coal. Ivana was always immaculate in home-made clothes and it was the delight of the teacher to send her to the bin knowing that she would be covered with coal dust upon her return. He mocked her every day, trying to defeat the faith so strongly entrenched in her heart.

On one particularly bitter winter day the schoolmaster was found to be in a very nasty mood. All the children were on alert to his desire to harm someone. He chose Ivana. Cheeks rosy from the winter wind, she entered the warm school with a cheery greeting and walked right into the hateful wrath of a man mad with hopelessness.

After ridiculing her before the students, he sent her outside without her coat, scarf, or mittens. He issued the edict that anyone helping her or even looking through the frosted window to know of her condition would join her. It was his intent to freeze the girl to death.

As the sister shared with me I could see the image of this frail preteen standing in the wind-driven snow and ice. My heart breaking, I asked her to continue.

They passed the day until 3 pm dismissal without a break. No one opened the door or looked out the window and at day's end they gathered up Ivana's coat, gloves, and scarf and went out to retrieve her body which must now be frozen.

There she was standing, hands lifted to heaven, worshipping the Lord. The grass at her feet was green and fresh as spring. Her skin was not cold at all. She was radiant in the power of the Lord. When they called to her and embraced her, she seemed to return from some far away place. She had no sense of time passing. She had been kept in the timeless warmth of the One in whom she believed.

All the school believed that day. The schoolmaster was transferred and life went on. But Ivana's story began to travel from school to school. The telling of it put hope in the hearts of students across Poland. By the time I traveled with her, there were 50,000 believers in the movement and it threatened to transform campuses across the land. After Ivana and I had worked together for the last time I asked her where she would go.

"Oh!" she exclaimed. "Some of my school friends have found a flat in East Berlin that faces the wall. We are all going to live there and pray around the clock until that wall comes down. We believe Jesus is going to set us free from the atheists from the east."

Ivana believes in a God who gives life. She had found the God who will sustain the oppressed and set the captive free. As I watched the footage of Ronald Reagan telling Mikhail Gorbachev to take down the wall, I could not help but wonder if God's camera was focused on a group of students in a little room on the east side calling on Him to do the same thing. Ivana is a believer. She acted upon her beliefs and she became the deliverer of thousands.

***

"What have you done?" The hat's questions came back to me.

"What have I done?" I asked deep within my heart. I am a believer; but what have I done to glorify the Lord in whom I believe? Do I follow and obey Him? Am I willing to risk my life to change nations?

My answer was surrounding the building. The sound of gunfire again brought me from the Old City to this small town in Indonesia. I looked at our group and thought, "Yes, we are believers. We would go the limit for the Lord we love."

Believers go out and proclaim a message

BELIEVERS go out and proclaim a message. They create cells or pockets of belief everywhere they go. The followers of Jesus circled the known world within 250 years of His ascension. The followers of Gautama Buddha have reached around the world also for the second century. Islam has taken the Book of the Prophet into every nation. Sitting in the cell in the world's largest Moslem nation I began to think that perhaps the world was getting too small for all of us to walk about with our beliefs. We will either have to agree to coexist in peace, or we will have to kill each other until none is left.

The thought drove my mind to the furthest point to which I had traveled to talk about Jesus. I am a believer. I travel to tell the story. I believe enough to act.

There is a nerve in your leg that cramps when you look up to see how far you have to climb. It happens on stairs and fire escapes. It happens on treadmills when you realize that only ten minutes have passed. But it really happens when you are trekking in the Himalayas.

We had been walking at a brisk pace up the hill from the gateway of Beni. Central Nepal is the trekking capital of the world and this trail is traveled by thousands each year. It takes you to the Annapurna Sanctuary, home of the world's most beautiful sunrise. It is known for its breathtaking reflection of the sun's early light. The path winds its way along a stumbling stream from 4,000 to 17,000 feet. The ascent takes days for foreigners so the route is dotted with guest houses at eight-hour intervals. We were on the way to the pass at Dharapani and looked forward to the hot springs along the way.

I saw him coming down the trail toward us. About ten minutes above, he had not yet recognized me. The nerve cramped and the breath fled from my lungs. Forcing myself to climb, I was energized by the thought of seeing this man. He was wearing the Penn State jersey I had given him and, with umbrella slung across razor-thin shoulders and scarf flung haphazardly about his neck, he looked for all the world like a movie set escapee.

Altering my pace and taking the middle of the path I waited for him to see the obstacle. Smiling gently, I looked up just as he stepped down to my level. His face filled with surprise and recognition.

"You are a terrible *guru*!" He exclaimed. "You are terrible. I threw off my old *guru* for you and you never came and gave me a word. I waited every day for your return and you never came."

"I am on my way to you now," I offered lamely. "And you will not be there when I arrive. Such a disappointment you have given me. Where are you going?"

"You told me to make believers of all the children I taught so I shared with them from the Book and they all believed. There is no more work for me to do on that mountain so I am going to the next mountain to tell them the good news. You said you would come and now, so late, you come to me." Joy filled his eyes at the thought of giving such a good report.

"I see you have kept the shirt," I offered.

"Yes, it is the mantle of my *guru*." He thrust back his shoulders to imitate my size.

"You look great," I said and sent him on his way, another believer going to great lengths to make other believers.

The first climb to his village had been somewhat difficult. In our desire to complete the lower loop of the Annapurna we had over-extended ourselves and were not able to make it to the Dharapani camp. We decided to pitch tent in a schoolyard and exchange some cash and gifts for the water and firewood. He had been the teacher, so we had great fun sharing English and telling riddles. Nepalese love riddles.

A large crowd of interested students had gathered to hear our conversation. A typical village teacher, he had become their key to understanding the world outside their high mountain perch. He translated my words for them and theirs for me and we had a wonderful evening. The students were very bright and had well-informed questions. One was about my traveling companion, Jim. He is an African American with white curly hair. I am a German American with blue eyes and a big belly.

They wanted to know why Americans came in so many shapes and sizes. They were very keen to try to rub off his black and my white and, to our delight we found that they felt related to him, but were foreign to me. How wonderful it was to have them peer deeply into our eyes and try to pull the hair from our legs. There is at least one place on earth where stereotypes have been eliminated.

As the evening drew to an end I asked the riddle, "I travel through the sky but I am not a plane or bird. I heal but I am not a doctor. I provide food, but I am not a farmer. Who am I?"

They worked and worked in small groups to determine the answer and finally reported, "No group can get all three and the groups cannot agree on answers to all three, so you must preserve peace by telling us the answer before we go home to bed."

The teacher finished translating the report and waited for the answer. Arms folded across his thin chest, chin thrust forward, he shared in the intrigue of the moment.

"The answer to the riddle is 'I am Jesus'," I said. "He heals the sick, He lives in the heavens. He gives us the food we eat. He is the answer to life's riddle." We all had a good laugh and away they went. The teacher remained at the tent flap until the children's voices had faded into the night.

"Is it real?" he asked. "Is it really Jesus who heals and who lives in the sky and who sends us the food?"

"Yes. It is He who loves you and gives you all you need." I watched his face as I answered.

"And you came here to speak for Him?" His question was sincere, not angry or offended.

"Yes, we believe He has sent us into all the world to tell people about Him." Jim answered in steady tones.

"Then it is true?" He turned to Jim. "It is really true, He lives in the sky, He heals the sick, He sends the food, and you are His disciples."

"Yes," we said together, looking to one another for leadership.

"You both believe it. He is for the white man and the black man?"

Ah, that was the point. The "White Man's God" had got some black skin.

"Then, if it is true, He can be my God and you my new friend shall be my *guru*." With that declaration he opened his neck bag, took out the picture of his old *guru* and gave us a big hug. "Now, tell me about the books you carry."

We introduced him to the Bible and, as the night wore on, he found solid faith in Jesus Christ. Can you imagine my joy when a year later I "bumped" into him on the trail from Beni. What are the odds of that happening? I tell you, my friend, that is God in action. He is the true God who sends us the food we need and who lives in the sky and who heals our diseases.

The true God does not tell us to kill those who do not believe as we do. He tells us to feed them. He tells us to bless them. He tells us to teach them what they will need to know for a better future. He is not afraid to be known by them. He is secure because He is true.

He said these signs would follow those who believe. They would be baptized, they would relieve the oppressed, they would speak in many languages, nothing would harm them and they would minister healing.

These are the signs that follow true believers of a true God and the greatest proof of the power of the truth is the transformation of people's lives. Jesus has made us ambassadors for healing, peace, and provision.

Ivana knew it. She became a believer and changed the course of the youth of her nation. This young teacher had found the truth that night and had made believers of the future generation of his village. The Nepalese who stormed us for the books had found it, as had the arresting officers.

$$* * *$$

Bolstered by this thought, I thought of the mob surrounding us and their desperate need for truth that would bring hope that would not make them ashamed. In my heart I cried out for them and then it dawned on me that 500 of them had received the truth that day.

I prayed that they would hide the books, wander away from the fighting, and seek the truth in those books. As we sat there wondering about our fate, my heart was encouraged at the thought of those young people believing in their hearts and moving from hate to help.

Believers take action. Believers go out. Believers change their nations.

CHAPTER EIGHT

The high hills

THE high hills of North Thailand are refuge to a hodgepodge of humanity. The porous border and rough terrain make it a haven for drug traffickers. The fresh breezes make it a sanctuary from the dank heat of the deltas. The high places make it perfect for spiritualists of all kinds to try to get closer to the Creator through His creation.

We had come to find a monk.

A young lady had come to one of our friends with terrible torment. She had not slept for days. Her mind was filled with thoughts of suicide and grotesque figures. Her voice had changed and her appearance was that of a modern zombie. Unkempt hair swept back to reveal a face developing deep lines of torment.

She had lost consciousness several times although a mandatory physical exam revealed nothing out of the ordinary. Doctors were puzzled, psychiatrists bemused, psychologists befuddled and she was brought to those known to be believers in Jesus.

We received her and surrounded her with a team of women who could pray for her night and day. We began to call upon the Lord for hope for her life and the ability to believe. The days were difficult, the nights terrifying.

As mental stability began to return she could eat some broth and drink some energy drinks. Once we could restore her physical balance she began to speak more clearly. Over a period of three months she began to tell a fascinating story of hate, revenge, spiritism and bondage. Some of it we immediately dismissed, only to recall later that she had shared those things with us. Her story, typical of a small group of women, but thought of by hundreds, taught us a great deal about the force of faith.

Married for several years, she had been a professional in the finance sector. Well educated and highly thought of in her profession, she and her husband appeared to be the model couple. Though they were not Christians or part of a local church, they did believe in and fear a god in heaven. Their marriage and careers were developing beautifully until the husband began to be away on business more frequently and for longer periods. Caught up in her career and trusting as she did, she did not investigate his absences for over a year. Then, at the suggestion of a friend, she began to ask questions on his return and it took less than six months for her to find out the truth, he was having an affair with another woman.

The discovery was devastating to her. Friends counseled that she not overreact, but she found this course impossible. Associates began to talk openly of her inability to keep her husband and the sharks of the marketplace began to close in on her client base. Soon her appearance began to change as sleep crept away into the dream world of torment.

The thought occurred to her to go to a temple and ask the spirits to regain her husband. She began to consult with temple mediums to gain the power to hold her husband. They were unable to make any change and always said she would have to go deeper into the spirit realm because the power of the other woman was very great. She drank potions, chanted curses, and made sacrifices to try to gain the upper hand but to no avail. Frustrated and deteriorating physically and mentally, she took leave of her business for a season and focused fully on this quest.

Through the mediums she heard of a monk in South Thailand who had special powers in cases like these. But, he was expensive and they did not know how he could be contacted. She booked a flight to the city where the man was said to be and began her search for him. Her appearance was a signboard of need. The local monks led her to mediums who led her to the man with the special powers.

She met with him several times, learned new chants, drank new potions, spent more money but to no avail. When she confronted the spiritist with the failure he commented that she had to believe in him and what they were doing. The answer was contingent upon her ability to believe. According to her testimony she tried everything she could to believe that this would work and her husband would return. Appetite gone, fasting was easy. Torment had taken her sleep, so recommended sleep deprivation also came naturally.

After 90 days of intensive sessions with the spiritist and thousands of dollars in offerings she was a skeleton. She had begun to take on the appearance of the spirits with which she had been communicating.

It was then that metal objects began to emanate from her skin. First there would be a bump and then a needle would emerge. This level of bondage is very rare even in Thai black magic. The spiritist began to withdraw from her; but at her insistence, agreed to enter a blood covenant with her. They drank each others blood mixed in wine and both placed their hands on a ceremonial cloth dedicated for the ritual. The blood mingled as did the spirits and they were bound to each other.

Shortly after this ceremony her friends committed her for psychiatric evaluation and the doctor referred her to a pastor and the case was referred to us. Our team included pastors and clinical psychologists from four nations. We agreed to take the case and based the activity in Kuala Lumpur, Malaysia. The pastor there was the lead with the rest of us consulting and supporting in prayer.

She made slow, steady progress, beginning to take food and get a little rest. Having no idea what her "right mind" would be, we just kept praying for the Lord to deliver her of all oppression. She could become violently angry and express a level of self abuse and hatred which was, at best, alarming to us. Each of us went through periods of wondering why and how we had gotten into this case, but the Lord's love for her kept us working on it.

As the spirit webs of her tormented mind began to unravel we could see a pathway of deliverance. We felt that the torment had begun in her inability to cope with the abandonment by her husband. When remorse turned to hate, she had opened her soul to torment. Her sense of failure was so profound that she had destroyed everything else in her life. She was suicidal in business, friendships, family, faith, and physically. Often she would try to cut her wrists.

Actually this became an encouragement to us because she always cut in the wrong direction and never deep enough to hit an artery so we felt that deep in her heart she did not want to die. Hope came with every onslaught.

Over 18 months more, we concluded that we needed to follow the story from medium to medium and break the curse through the power of Jesus' name. So we started the search that would bring us to the hilltop of North Thailand.

The first stop, local temples in Singapore, was very simple. More tourist than belief, they remembered the case and said in one voice, "South Thailand."

We met in North Malaysia and drove up to Thailand. Along the way she began to have a desperate episode so we had to slow the pace and encourage her to have the faith to face the torment in her soul. We searched the city. Yes, they knew her and the man she had been meeting. He was gone. His "temple" had been burned to the ground by a husband who found out that the medium was using black magic against him. Some felt the spiritist had died in the fire, others were not sure.

After two days we found a medium that the lady recognized as having assisted in one of the events and he directed us to North Thailand. The man we were looking for was building a new temple on one of the high hills.

We flew to Chiang Mai, got a couple of vehicles and a translator for the Hill Tribes. Leck, a Karen Pastor and solid believer in Jesus, joined our team to help us communicate in the high hills. We drove up there in two vehicles. Always watching the lady for some sign of recognition in the spirit we were amazed to see that she slept well on the trip. It looked like the closer we got to the man the calmer she became. Fearing that she would slip off the other side into a deep trance we tried to balance her through unrelated conversation.

We arrived in the town at about 11 am and took a walk about to see if we could find a contact to the man. The place is filled with all nationalities; Chinese who fled to freedom, hippies from the world over, Thai and Burmese, and the local Hill Tribes. Stopping at a local church we found a Chinese pastor who told us of the coming from the South of a very strong medium who appeared to have quite a bit of money. He showed us the location of the new facility the man was building and said that many of his church members and those of other churches had begun to believe in the man. This fellow, he said, was very powerful in the ancient arts of Thai Black Magic and there were cases already in the villages where anyone who opposed him had become violently ill and some had died.

Following his direction and excusing him from participation, we went to find this man. It was a beautiful day in one of the world's most spectacular places. The day was so clear that it made an impression upon us. We were on peaks several hundred feet above the valleys. The hillsides were covered with verdant foliage. Multicolored parrots sped their way from tree to tree and the sound of song birds filled the crisp clean air. Only one little cloud clung to the valley floor. Perhaps shaded from the sun, or fed by a bamboo cluster, it had escaped the morning's heat.

The monk was building quite a facility. He indeed had some money. About 20 novitiates were there to serve him. His main building was steel and sheet metal. They were just constructing the altar and it was immense. The idol had not yet been made; but the base on which it would stand was 20 by 10 meters. This man had a following somewhere.

We left the lady in the van with two women and asked for the monk. Hopeful of an offering from a Westerner, he came toward us with the sheepish smile common to Asian beggars. Hands extended and then elevated in prayer he greeted each of our team. Finally coming to me he asked Leck who we were and what we wanted. We had instructed Leck to tell him that I was a "fat holy man from the West," that I had heard of his powers, and that I had come to exchange some fortune telling with him. The young man was to say that I had a "word" for this man and that I felt that he would have a "word" for me. We were hoping for a face to face, in the spirit, meeting.

He was very happy to oblige and we sat together with tea. I suggested he go first and so he went into a trance and then told me that I was great in the spirit, had good karma, was free to walk throughout Asia and would have no trouble; but to watch out for the Arabs as they would try to kill me.

When it was my turn, I looked deep into his eyes and then spoke in tongues. After a few minutes, when he had crossed from nervousness to realizing something real was happening here, I took his hand in mine. Then I told him that he had been having a recurring dream. He could see the end of the age was coming. He could see the devastation and a face kept appearing to him. He did not know the name of the person. The face had been beaten and the forehead cut as if with thorns. Blood flowed on the face.

He knew in his spirit that if he could call the name of the man with the face, he would be saved from the fires that were consuming everything. But he was awakened without knowing the name. I asked if it was true and he said yes.

Then, holding his right hand in mine, I told him I knew the name and had been sent to tell him. I asked if he wanted to know the name. He said of course he did.

I told him that once he knew this name he could no longer call upon any other name. This name is the only name he would ever be able to call or he would perish in the fires he had seen. I asked again if he wanted to know the name. Yes, of course he did. At this point his eyes were twitching and he was beginning to sweat.

Leck positioned himself close to the man. I held his hand and, leaning forward, told him that the man he had seen, the man who could save him from the fire, the man with the piercing eyes and the blood flowing from his face, was none other than Jesus.

When Leck said the name Jesus several things happened. The man pulled his hand free and struck the young pastor twice across the face before jumping to his feet and cursing us. He stormed about the place screaming, "Never say that name! Never say that Name!"

Trying to light a cigarette he dismissed the young students, and in a complete rage began to move toward the two of us. The wind began to blow and suddenly, over the edge of the mountain came the little cloud. Now a great whirlwind, it swept through the place where we were. It blew away every loose thing and several of our group and the young monks fell to their knees in fear. The power was like nothing I have ever seen.

From his knees Leck offered this prayer, "Father, forgive him."

The monk/medium/spiritist ran to his house and cursed us from inside. Feeling that the power had been driven from him we left.

Our next stop was the hilltop temple of the King of Thailand. We went there and prayed for the beautiful country. During this time three gangsters came to confront the Karen Pastor. They threatened his life if we returned. At peace with it all, we left.

The next morning, a Pastor in Chiang Mai came to greet us. He had heard about the whirlwind and wanted to show us the morning paper. There had been, at exactly the same time, very powerful winds blowing through Chiang Mai. And, the paper went on to say, very strange occurrences as whirlwinds blew through all of the north-eastern section of Thailand.

In the years that have followed, revival has come to those villages. Many miracles have happened but, in particular, curses and Thai Black Magic have been stopped.

The lady has been healed. She does not look like she did before it all happened. Those who know her say she is more radiant a person that she had ever been. Her husband has not returned, and may never return; but, through the power of the Name of Jesus, she is free.

The young Pastor who took the hit continues to disciple those who believe.

The monk/medium/spiritist was gunned down by gangsters several months later.

✳✳✳

Gunfire is the last futility of man in expressing his desire to control. It was true in Thailand and it is true in Aceh. When the guns come out, reason has stopped.

In our situation things were becoming unreasonable.

CHAPTER NINE

The walls were beginning to close in on us

The walls were beginning to close in on us. Accustomed to walking about, I was beginning to feel the need to stretch my legs. To the left of the cell was an open court about three by three meters. It had a sink and some buckets, obviously the custodian's washroom. Leaving the enclosure, I walked out into this area only to hear more clearly the sounds of the conflict outside. We had been about an hour and a half into the event and the crowd had not lost any of its fury, a barrage of stones and bottles flew into the courtyard and I realized that the open roof made it a point of possible access to our refuge. As I stepped quickly back inside, I thought of believers who I know have spent long times in such places.

***

I thought of Alan Yuan and his 20 years of hard labor in the far west regions of China. He was in a place so bleak that there were no walls. The guards would tell them to leave any time they wanted to. They were completely surrounded by the Turkmen Desert and no one could survive.

I thought of Wang Ming Dao and his 22-year-and-10-month honeymoon with Jesus. His crime was to refuse, as Alan had, to sign allegiance to the Communist Party in China. He had thought of suicide, but the Lord had preserved him.

I thought of our own previous arrests in China, Nepal, Mongolia, and Russia, and how the Lord had always come through for us. But now my mind went to Pastor Mai, a dear friend from Vietnam.

With the fall of Saigon and the reeducation program of the Communists, all those who believed in Jesus had to renounce their faith or agree to not spread it. In Saigon City there was a group of young seminarians who had divergent opinions on what was the expedient thing to do. One group thought that a live dog is better than a dead lion and following that proverb, agreed. Through them the church, though severely compromised, was given recognition by the government. Although they were not able to grow the church through the occupation, they were able to outlast the oppression and survive.

The second group thought it best to go underground and resist as long as they could. This group was led by four young men who had experienced the Pentecostal Baptism in the Holy Spirit. To say they were close with the first group would not be true. They had their differences and were viewed as fanatic and extreme.

The problem came when the first group gave information to the government concerning the second group. What pressures were applied to exact that information we do not know, but it was given and the four members of the underground group were sought out, arrested, and tortured to deny their faith and sign with the party. None of them ever did. A man I often think about when I am under pressure for the cause of Christ is Pastor Mai, one of those men.

With his church closed, and having been branded as a rebel, Mai began to meet in a home. He had 17 followers, including his family. They often had to change their meeting places. They had a very intense love for worship, the Bible, and each other. The pressure of the day was the crucible from which they would eventually emerge indivisible.

Someone gave information to the police about the group and their meetings. To this day, no one has confessed or apologized concerning this, so it is left to the unknown; but, the police came and took Mai for questioning.

When he refused to cooperate, they advanced the interrogation to less humane means. They passed through solitary confinement and he would not give them the names of his members. They tried beatings and he would not give names. They tried food and sleep denial and he would not give names. So, in frustration, they tied his hands behind his back and hung him on a peg in the wall in a totally dark room and left him there to break or die.

The pain never let up. He cried out to the Lord in tongues with every waking moment. Days passed. The guards listened to the shouting become more and more muffled until it was a murmur. They declared him insane and threw him out into an alley behind the jail thinking he would surely die.

After days in the total dark and with energy coming only from the Lord, Mai managed to wriggle his way into a doorway to wait for nightfall. His arms were severely damaged by the treatment and he was famished for water, so he drank what he could find and made his way home. There, in the loving arms of his wife and home church, he mended. On that day his church was 17 people.

I was introduced to him by a mutual friend. We had prayed our way through Vietnam and had come to Saigon on our way back to Singapore. My friend arranged the meeting, telling the people that I too had been arrested several times for my faith and that they would find good fellowship. They also mentioned the South East Asia Prayer Center and our commitment to local house church movements. The meeting was arranged.

We became fast friends. I was invited to return and teach the following year in a leaders' retreat to be held at a beach location. Honored beyond imagination, I set my schedule by that meeting.

On the first day I was standing in the gentle surf with a Vietnamese Pastor a few years my junior. As the waves gently swept the sand from our legs he deftly reached into the water and retrieved a long strand of kelp. Biting off a section for himself, he offered the rest to me. In like fashion to his, I bit off a big piece and handed it back to him. Amazed, he took another bite and grinned as he chewed. Not to be put off, I again followed and the process continued until he indicated he had had enough.

"Where you meet Mai?" he asked, while chewing the last mouthful.

"Friend of a friend," I answered.

"We meet in jail," he went on, satisfied with my knowledge of the standard house church answer.

"He told me about Jesus." He continued looking up the beach toward the Pastor. "He a good man, lead many to Jesus."

That evening, under the cover of a netted canopy strung from palm to palm, I heard some of the most fascinating testimonies of believers. Most of the key leaders had come to Christ while in prison. They were people who had worked for or been related in some way to the Americans. It was assumed that they were collaborators in the counter revolution. They had been imprisoned on political grounds and had been mixed in with the four Christian leaders.

One by one they shared their stories of release, beginning to share the word of God, recapture for illegal meetings or reeducation, release, preaching and so forth. Men and women shared with candor their extreme faith in Jesus. My own belief level paled in the light of their passion.

It became clear that night that one believer, hung on a wall to die; had resulted in the conversion of 40,000 people; and, that those people were very closely knit and traveled throughout Vietnam carrying the good news of Jesus Christ.

We were joined by the Lion of Danang. A young lady, she was the daughter so many of them had lost. She had just been released from a Haiphong jail after being arrested for preaching Christianity. How did they know she was from Danang? Her accent. A policeman had overheard her asking directions and knew she was not local and brought her to the neighborhood station to find out where she was from and what she was doing out of her area. She was identified by previous record and had spent a month in jail. She was most animated as she shared testimony after testimony of those who had come to Christ in the jail. The Lord had turned her difficult situation into a time of harvest and victory. She had not felt fear at all.

I was reminded of Peter being identified as a Galilean by the little girl at the fireside and how he had tried to deny his belief in Christ. This young woman had reversed the tables. She was so very bold. They discussed her next travel and decided to send her farther north to the China border to confirm the reports they had heard from that area.

Their next matter was the discussion of criteria for the title "full-time worker." For them this involved selling home and lands, giving that money to the treasury of the work, and striking out by faith to plant a church where there was none.

✳✳✳

As I remembered all this, I looked around at our team. Sure, we were committed to Christ. Yes, of course we believed enough to hear from Him and obey what He was asking us to do. But, which one of us could take the steps these people had taken. I was humbled then and I am humbled now. Their commitment has kept the flame of faith burning brightly through an otherwise dark day in the life of the church in Asia. They expressed, under the cover of darkness, a level of commitment I had never known. My embarrassment grew as I realized that after the reports, I was to share my faith with them.

Perhaps it was the sound of the gunfire, the arms locker in the hall way, the smell of the gun smoke, or the sound of the helicopter in the air, my mind was not in Indonesia in 1999, it was clearly in Vietnam 25 years before. Mai had "survived," so would we. The Lion had "survived," so would we. And, if the Lord was going to allow us to be tortured, then we would join with a happy group afterwards to share the fellowship of His suffering.

Leck had said of the blow to his face, "I thank God that He has counted me worthy to suffer today for His name's sake. I ask Him to forgive the man and save his soul."

Ivana had prayed daily for the schoolmaster who had tried to commit her to a painful death. One day she explained to me, "We do not hate the Russians any more than our parents hated the Germans. We pray for them; and, should the Lord desire that we suffer to draw closer to Him, then we thank God for the honor to suffer in His name."

There was the sound of a group of people coming down the hallway. I looked at the Banker. He held up five fingers and I thought, "What will this be?"

"Be Wise as Serpents and Harmless as Doves"

Matthew 10:16-26

[16]"Behold, I send you out as sheep in the midst of wolves. Therefore be wise as serpents and harmless as doves. [17]But beware of men, for they will deliver you up to councils and scourge you in their synagogues. [18]You will be brought before governors and kings for My sake, as a testimony to them and to the Gentiles. [19]But when they deliver you up, do not worry about how or what you should speak. For it will be given to you in that hour what you should speak; [20]for it is not you who speak, but the Spirit of your Father who speaks in you.

[21]"Now brother will deliver up brother to death, and a father his child; and children will rise up against parents and cause them to be put to death. [22]And you will be hated by all for My name's sake. But he who endures to the end will be saved. [23]When they persecute you in this city, flee to another. For assuredly, I say to you, you will not have gone through the cities of Israel before the Son of Man comes.

[24]"A disciple is not above his teacher, nor a servant above his master. [25]It is enough for a disciple that he be like his teacher, and a servant like his master. If they have called the master of the house Beelzebub, how much more will they call those of his household! [26]Therefore do not fear them. For there is nothing covered that will not be revealed, and hidden that will not be known.

CHAPTER TEN

It was a small group

IT was a small group. The slight man with the gun in his waistband, a uniform, and a small man with a round head. They were polite, asked if we were alright, and assured us that the situation had intensified.

The small, round-headed man was introduced as an officer from Interpol. He was very professional. He stood with the air of authority one would expect.

"Mr. Mark," he began the explanation that has stuck with me through these years. "This has become an international situation. I am certain that you had no idea where you were or what was happening here when you arrived. I am sure you understand more about it now. Because you are from the USA, this situation has very strong international implications. Eventually, your government will become involved as well as the government of your friend. Please cooperate with these men in every way. They are professionals and will help you in this situation. We will be in contact with your governments to assure them of your safety and answer any questions they may have. I am sure that with your cooperation this matter can be resolved."

The slight man was next. He had been changing into a black shirt while the other man spoke. He had no fat. He was the build of a Siamese cat and had the same eyes. He stood before me and looked through my eyes to my soul as he spoke.

"Mr. Mark," he was gentle in his speech. "I am what we call in the police here a 'Ninja'. This is a term used for those of us who are authorized to use our bodies as weapons and who can kill without permission. We answer to no one. It is my job to see that you and your friends are not killed. The people outside have demanded that you be turned over to them. Then you would be tortured, torn limb from limb, and dragged through the streets. They honestly hate you.

"Do not worry. You will be alright. Just do exactly as we say. It is our job to protect you and we will. I am going out to talk with them and try to get them to see that you are not worth dying for."

As he left, the uniform stepped up. His calm was my joy.

"Mr. Mark, I am in charge of the uniformed police and the military involved in this international situation. Did you hear the sound of the helicopter? We tried to fly a chopper in here to take you out, but when it approached the area someone in the crowd lifted a surface-to-air device. Thankfully it was spotted and the chopper withdrew or they would have shot it down. If that had happened, they would have gained the courage to rush the building and kill us all. This is a very serious situation.

"It is no longer important whether or not you knew the situation here. What is important now is that we get you and my people out of here alive. The power to the station has been cut. Your car has been burned. The rioters have gained access to the building two times.

"We are having the commandos come to rescue us. It will take at least 45 minutes for them to get here. Please stay away from the windows and follow any orders we give you."

As they turned and went to their respective stations we all looked at the Banker. He was holding up six fingers. We smiled to each other and took our places of waiting. There was no talk, no *verbal prayer. It wasn't like any other life-threatening time I had ever experienced. We were all filled with a resolute calm.*

It was then that I realized that I was prepared to meet Jesus. "I could be a martyr of the faith in just a couple of hours," I thought as I turned back to my waiting place.

Other people had threatened to kill me before. There was the man who was a wife-beater who came to my office with the .357 magnum and threatened to blow my brains out if I didn't tell him where his wife was. I didn't. He didn't and even when he got out of jail, he didn't.

There was the Catholic priest in Guatemala who assured me I would be dead in the morning if another young person prayed with me to receive Jesus.

But those things had happened quickly; this was taking a lot of time. It gave me time to prepare my heart. Jesus began to prepare me as He has all those who have been sent out by Him. He promised, "After the Holy Ghost is come upon you, you will receive power to be martyrs for me."

I returned to my corner of the room and felt that sweet presence come upon me. Again there was no fear, just a certain looking forward to the chapters of the plan of God as they would unfold in my life.

CHAPTER ELEVEN

"Love your enemies"

Jesus said, "Love your enemies." Were these Indonesians, so hungry for our blood, really our enemies? Had we not instigated the whole thing? How should I feel about a couple of thousand people who wanted to "Cut me limb by limb and drag me through the streets?"

Did they represent all Moslems? Were they just so frustrated with the imbalance of wealth? Were they that fearful of three middle-aged men and a youth? Was America that bad, really? Were they under the influence of evil spirits? Were we pawns in an international opportunity to be on CNN? These thoughts and more flooded my mind as I sat down to wait out the next chapter.

Level six; the Banker said we had reached level six. I realized a new keen awareness of sounds. There was a discernible calm among us. The Doctor's veins were calm and, without the driver's nervousness, we could almost take a nap. We shared tense smiles, raised eyebrows, shoulder shrugs all around and a gentle smile for our guide. It was all in a day's work for those sent out by the Lord. We were a team. There were no divisions. We had been called of the Lord to share a common experience and, while it was not what we had in mind in the morning, it made for a very interesting afternoon.

"Love your enemy." Christian maturity is seen in this simple sentence and I rested my drifting mind on its anchor. Would a person who was going to kill you be seen as your enemy?

✳✳✳

WE had walked for three days along the Dudh Kosi River in the Terai region of the Royal Kingdom of Nepal. It was hot and the torrential rains that fell did nothing to cool that heat. Our team of four Westerners and four Nepalese had been dropped from a truck in the middle of the night, had turned upriver the next morning and had been walking ever since. We had made 17 river crossings and had spent hours sloshing along through flooded rice paddies. Our first night we had dispossessed a horse from her bedding place only to lose to her countermove at about 3 in the morning. We had blisters. We had no good food. We had 19 days of uphill trekking before us and we were not in a good mood.

Befriended by a dashing young leader on horseback, we were led to his family's grain mill where we enjoyed a mid-day nap and some fresh water. With only four hours to go we headed into the town of Ghaigat, Sagarmatha Province. This little town had a school and food, and we were glad to reach it. The kids from the school lightened our bags of several copies of, "Who is Jesus." Everyone was happy.

Except, that is, a lawyer standing across the street. He made a beeline for one of the kids, took the book, and headed for the police. Our team took a vote and decided to sit it out in a tea shop. We got some rice and started to refill our empty tanks when the commotion began. The lawyer was back, and this time with the law. Eight of us went eight directions as quickly as we could. They decided to follow me. It was a good choice; I was the oldest, the fattest, and the slowest in the team.

I was ok till we hit an uphill, which in Nepal is about every 50 meters. Our guide/translator was with me. Maybe they wanted to talk to him and I was just in the bargain. The policeman put his hand on my shoulder and softly said, "Would you come with me please?"

I have since learned that the gentleness with which this is said does not always indicate the strength of the person saying it. Some very big policemen have very gentle voices.

Slowly turning I submitted to his direction. He was tall, in his early 20s and thrilled that he had done his duty to preserve public safety. Not a bad kid at all, he wanted to practice his English so we worked on basketball vocabulary. I am often amazed at the penetration of professional sports around the world. People who do not know about flush toilets can tell you who won last year's slam dunk contest. And in the days of Michael Jordan, the world was awash in Nike imitations. Every police outpost I have visited from Siam to Siberia has a tattered basketball hoop and this one was no exception. This young man could never be called, "your enemy."

As we approached the building housing the municipal court and the chief district officer's office the young man stopped me for a very formal briefing. "This man you are about to meet is the Chief District Officer of this district. He holds the power of life and death over everyone who lives here. When we go in I will bow down on the floor before him to show respect. You must bow down also and wait for him to say to you to get up. Do not raise your eyes before he tells you to."

Now, I thought, we are approaching someone who has too high a self image and hell will freeze over before I bow down to a Chief District Officer in this time-forgotten hole-in-the-wall town.

We entered an austere room and sure enough the policeman hit his knees in front of the desk. I smiled courteously and extended my hand to the man I would come to love.

"Rise," he said to the policeman who was amazed that I was standing.

"Stand by," he again directed his comment to the young man.

"Good," I thought. "He is a man of few words. Now he will tell me something and I will leave and that will be the end of that."

"Mr. Mark." His eyes rose from my passport. His English was with a British accent. "You have caused me a big problem today. Has our officer informed you as to my rank and title in this District? You know that this is my District and I hold the power of life and death here? Your future is in my hands.

"Please come and sit here. Bring us some tea. Would you like a biscuit? That will be all."

The room emptied of all but the police officer and the servant who brought tea and biscuits and made us most comfortable. I began to like this man. Maybe he had to have such a fierce front to keep the locals in check. I had no idea, but the gentleman was much nicer than the life-and-death king.

"Now, as I say, you have caused me a big problem today. Do you know that Nepal is a Hindu country? That is to say that everyone in Nepal is a Hindu and our King is descended from a Hindu god."

I had no idea about any such thing. There are Buddhists and there are Moslems and there are Christians so I thought his point of view to be pretty narrow. Seeing the question in my eyes, he continued his explanation.

"All Nepalese are registered. If you are born in a Hindu

family, then you are Hindu. If you are born in a Buddhist family, then you are Buddhist. Do you understand?"

Not waiting for an answer, he continued. "Did you know that to change one's religion you have to re-register and you could spend one year in jail? Did you know that when you re-register you must supply the name of the person who convinced you to change religion and that person must spend three years in jail? And, did you know that if you change your religion to Christianity and you are baptized in water you must spend six years in jail and the person who persuades you to change your religion and to be baptized must spend six years in jail for every person?"

"I did not know," I answered.

"I thought you did not know so I got you this copy of our law in English so that you would not be ignorant of the law. Please tell me what you did last night."

"I had some rotten rice, ate a piece of cheese and slept." I sipped my tea.

"Yes, but before that you told 200 Nepalese to repeat a prayer and change their religion and you gave them a book. And, because you are a white Westerner, these innocent people believed you and prayed with you and now they all want to re-register as Christians. You have given me a big problem. You must go to jail for three years per person or a total of 600 years." He was not smiling.

"Now, tell me, why did you come here?" He sat back to listen to the only defense I could give in the face of evidence and a clear case of proselytizing.

"Sir," I began with respect after a deep draught of tea to clean my tightening throat. "It was never my intention to cause you any problem. Actually, the problem began when you arrested me. If I had not been arrested, there would be no problem; but to the bigger question of 'why did I come here?'...

"I am a believer in Jesus Christ. He is the Love of God demonstrated for all men. He has asked us to go into all the earth to tell everyone that if they will believe in Him they will have eternal life. If they call upon His name they will be saved. I found this to be true in my life. I was caught in sins that I could not defeat through discipline or self control. I called upon the Lord and He heard me and delivered me from this sin.

"It is His love that compels us to go to every man and give him the opportunity to be saved. Look at me, Sir. I am too old for this trekking and I am not at all fit for it; but, because Jesus loves you, I have walked all this way.

"Jesus knows who you are. Jesus knows where you are. And, Jesus knows what you need. Because He loves you, He has sent us here to tell you. He probably controlled even our arrest so that you might know that He loves you.

"It is not as if we had chosen Nepal to the exclusion of others. We have walked in many nations and will walk in still more, if you allow it, to tell people about Jesus and His great love for them."

Having delivered the message I sat back and watched his face.

"This," he said, "gives me a really big problem. I am the law in this district. All my people know that, there is no question. You have broken the law. If I put you in jail your country will come and get you and my people will say I bowed the knee to the U.S. If I do not put you in jail my people will say I am a weak ruler and I bowed my knee to the foreigner. This is a big problem. What am I to do with you?"

Silence is a great defense. I looked at him with true compassion for his dilemma.

"I could just have my men take you out to a cliff and throw you off and report you as a trekking accident. We have those here every year."

We shared some more tea and glucose biscuits as he read the "evidence" taken by the lawyer. He was intent on unraveling the dilemma and I saw no need to interrupt his study. Finally, he straightened his desktop, leaned forward in his chair and fixed his eyes on mine.

"I have decided to show you grace. I will let you go if you promise that you will not share this book with any more people in my district." He seemed satisfied so I got out my map to see where the end of his district was. It was a two-day walk for me, one day for his young policeman who was going to go with us to be certain no local person tried to bother us with conversation. Deal struck, we had tea and our team spent the night with company from the police force.

We trekked on through Nepal and found great receptivity for the message we carried. I met wonderful policemen and military along the way. We got to stay in the police station in two towns and a military jail in a third. It was very eye opening.

The following year I was in Kathmandu and was approached by a local Christian leader. He had heard of my arrest and zeal for the gospel and he excitedly shared with me a clipping from the front page of the Kathmandu newspaper. The CDO of the town of Ghaigat had been struck dead by a bolt of lightning from a clear blue sky. Local believers had seen it as a sign from heaven and, caught up in it all, I began to share that it was not wise to handle servants of God in a negative way.

Six months later, while preparing to share this story I was reminded of the love the Lord had for this man whose task it was to prevent others from becoming Christians. He had arranged for me to go. The timing was perfect, to be arrested and to share His love with the CDO knowing that within the year he would die.

The power of life and death was not with the man with the title, it was with the One who gave His life that all may live.

Perhaps it was the comment of the Ninja about the right to kill, or the comment of the police and military concerning our outcome, but this remembrance gave me great joy. Love your enemies and pray for those who spitefully use you (Matthew 5:43-45).

The ones who are our enemies

"**B**ut, you could not understand, we will always be poor." Hector's words cut to my heart. We stood on the rim of the "Limonada," a barrio in Guatemala famous for crime. These people do not want to do drugs, they do not want to steal, they certainly do not want to die young; but that is life for us and it will never change. We do not have one drop of hope it will change."

"Brother Mark," he continued with a smile. "You love us. We can feel that you love us. You can walk anywhere down there and be safe because the people know you love them. But, other people who come here, the fat cats and rich, they are the ones who are our enemies. They keep us living like this through the power of their money and corruption. They control the drugs and the crime. They take the youngest kids and make them addicts, thieves, prostitutes and murderers. Then they treat us like the filth they have caused us to become.

"If one of them ever comes down here, he would be killed for his shoes. Brother, we are born to this, and we will die to it. They will never allow this system to change. They are the enemies of their own people. There is no changing the fact of one's name. When I put my address as here, the job is gone. When I give my "two-name" name, people know I have no father, the doors are closed.

"Brother, we have a caste system here. Even in the church. If you and I go to a meeting everyone will want to be near you because you are from North America and I am from the 'limonada.' I will be asked to stay outside the door while you can go in. You will be free to talk with anyone in the room, I cannot. It is the way of life for us. We accept it. We do not hate you for it, it is the system. It will not change for us. Not now, not ever."

✳✳✳

Was this how they felt out in that street? Was this the fire that burned in the Irate Imam and the "Ball Cap?" Was this why they shook with the desire to kill and talked about cutting off our limbs and dragging us through the streets? Had the crumbs of the tilted table so offended them that they were willing to risk their own lives just to be somebody?

How I understood as I listened to their chanting from my safe waiting place. "Love your friends, hate your enemies" was the message of so many books. "Get even for what they have done to us!" "They think they are superior, they do not recognize our culture, they do not recognize the prophet, death to the infidels." These were the logs on the fire; but had the spark been something deeper?

✳✳✳

On that afternoon in Guatemala I had forced my young friend into my truck and we had driven to the National Palace. With him in tow I used all of my white North

American courage and walked right past the guards and into the foyer. I took the steps two a time, reaching the reception room of the President before anyone could ask why. Staying close to me, he was amazed as I opened the door and said to the guard, "Turn on the lights."

Hector was in shock when I had him come with me to the platform where the President's chair was and had him sit in the forbidden seat of power. The guard looked a bit surprised when I handed him the camera and had him take the photo that will forever be in my memory. "Jesus has caused us to sit in heavenly places high above all principalities and powers."

My young friend had just learned the first lesson of loving your enemies. Do not have any enemies.

For the next 20 years Hector fought the battle to rise above the racial discrimination with which he had been born. The injustices have been many. I have watched people completely ignore him in a room. This man who has founded churches, given thousands for the poor, established his own business and successfully run it, raised three children as a widower while supporting his mother and an invalid sister, is often treated as a lesser being by people who were born in a different zone or country. I have seen the pain in his heart and the agony on his face as he watches others of lowly estate become the downtrodden masses of humanity.

✳✳✳

Was this the fuel for the cry in the Aceh streets that day? As I sat in my cell and thought about it, I realized that just as the Army of the Poor would load a group of gunmen on a pickup truck and chase medical care from their community, so would the Irate Imam and the Baseball Cap chase investment, medicine, and education from theirs. They would rather be sick, dumb, and poor than have to sit any longer under the rich man's table. Social reform was the cry in the streets and they felt that Allah could give it to them if they could just rid the place of infidels and those who gave them sanctuary.

Were they the "enemy?"

Was I the "enemy?"

We were talking about killing. The "Ninja" represented us. He would speak for us and his right to kill was the extension of our being there. Who would die first for us?

The surface-to-air weapon was not what one would bring to a religious debate. This thing had deeper roots. Why would a man pull on an "I Love America" shirt and that stupid-looking hat and then lecture me on religion. What was going on here? Was it an uprising in the centuries-old ethnic dispute of the Acehnese and the Javanese? Why the reference to Ambon where Christians and Moslems were slaughtering each other every night in the name of their gods?

Who was the "enemy?"

I have faced death many times. No stranger to the feel of its presence, I am very alert when it is around. Someone was going to die this day. Someone was going to be slain by an "enemy," which is to say a person taking an opposite position. It could be me, but probably it would be some kid who decided to try the "Ninja" or who didn't move when the commandoes came through to get us.

✳✳✳

In my first year as a missionary I contracted malaria. Some little mosquito carried it to me. I have no idea if he escaped, but the disease became my life-threatening enemy. We fought it with medicine and blankets and rubbing alcohol and all that goes into the war with this enemy. I lost weight, was violently ill, was confined to bed, and vomited at the smell of any food. The fevers and chills chased each other for possession of my body.

Outside our group home was a Spanish man. I later came to know that his name was Felipe Gonzales. He was born in Guatemala and was Pastor to the youth who lived in the *Limonada*. He heard I was sick and began fasting and praying for my healing. Each day he came and walked and prayed in front of the house. As he passed he would touch the door and the bell but would neither knock nor sound the bell.

One day our young team-mate, Jonathan, said, "This man comes every day, but he does not knock. Should I ask him in?"

"Certainly," I said, wondering what this would be about.

Felipe entered the room very apologetically and asked general questions about my health and the family and so forth. Finally I asked him if he would pray for me.

"Me, pray for you?" he asked.

"Yes, please, would you pray for me?" I responded not realizing that he had never in his life felt worthy to pray for a white missionary.

As he prayed I felt warmth cover my entire body. Something touched me. Something healing touched me and, within a week, I was in wonderful shape. The malaria was gone and has never returned.

What had been the "enemy?" Was this man so culture-bound that I could have laid there and died without his prayers? Had we done this to him?

There is an enemy. He is ready to add fuel to any burning offence. He will always couch his deceptions in religious or spiritual terms. He comes to rob, to hurt, to kill and to destroy. People are taken captive to his ways when they harbor resentments or when they are oppressed into believing that they are lesser. Often, they feel as the disciples did that some day a deliverer will come who will lift the heel of the oil company or the existing government or the religious hierarchy from their throat.

The disciples of Jesus wanted to be free from Rome. They wanted a kingdom to be established on the earth in which they would sit at the right and left hands of the King and they would rule. This was their dream and when it looked like Jesus could not deliver it, they all fled. They all ran away. They were scattered from a false hope.

But Jesus came to give them the victory over the one who was the enemy of their souls. Not distracted by economics and politics, Jesus remained focused on the task before Him. He suffered the cross, taking the hatred of every man...even those in the Aceh street, the "Ninja", the Irate Imam, and the "Baseball Cap."

Jesus defeated the real enemy when He rose from the dead. Is it any wonder those who teach "an eye for an eye" also teach that Jesus was not really on the cross. Is it any wonder that those who teach "a tooth for a tooth, a limb for a limb, take vengeance for your position in life," also teach that there is no resurrection from the dead; that if it was Jesus on the cross, then He stayed in the grave and the disciples faked it. Is it any wonder that instead of teaching young men to heal they teach them to kill?

No, those in the street were not the enemy.

The guards at the palace were not the enemy.

The door and the bell were not the enemy.

The enemy is that spirit that turns man against man. It is that spirit that does not see the value of each individual. It is that one who robs, hurts, kills, and destroys. Jesus came that we might have life, and have it more abundantly. That means sitting in His chair. That means healing for all. That means an open heart to every man. That means striving for unity, not divisions among men.

CHAPTER THIRTEEN

The "Dominoes" will fall

THE "Dominoes" will fall in Latin America. The same way Communism has swept through Europe and is sweeping through Asia, it will now sweep through Latin America until the hammer and sickle rest on American shores. This was the mantra of the masses as we entered Guatemala. Their only hope is found in land reform. The Indians have the right to rule themselves and be free from the Yankee oppressors. Che Guevara and Uncle Fidel are the only hope for the miserable multitudes. First will be Nicaragua, then El Salvador and Honduras, and then Guatemala before the prize, Mexico.

As though sparked by this cacophony of false hope, the earth shook. It shook violently for about 35 seconds. The epicenter was in a little arid valley on the small river Motagua which drains whatever water might fall off the dry side of the continental divide as it winds its way through the former Mayan wonder now known as Guatemala. It really shook. From side to side and up and down the earth opened to swallow the lives of 50,000 people in 35 seconds.

Survivors tell that dogs wandered out in the streets and dropped dead from shock. All of creation shook as if

God had picked up a corner of the earth's surface and given it a hard shake. Women became widows, children became orphans and villages became graveyards in that instant. Hopes and dreams were shattered and politics went out with the screams of those trapped beneath mountains of rubble.

One of those trapped beneath the rubble was Lazuro Ochoa Catalan. Don Lacho, as he was affectionately known in his village, was an old man. He was from the Catalan/Mayen family line that had lived on the southern rim of the Motagua valley for generations. Unlike the shorter, broader, dark-eyed Mayans, these descendants of the Conquistadores were tall with green and brown eyes and fair skin. He had been asleep when the dark village was shaken. The roof caved in. Struck in the head by a terra cotta roof tile, he laid in an increasing pool of his own blood. He later said that through his time lying trapped and dazed, he despaired of the hope of lasting through that fateful night.

Hector Zetino was a teenager. His father was gone and he lived in a corrugated tin shack perched on a steep hillside in one of the barrios of impoverished multitudes in the capital of Guatemala. A gangster, he was used to surviving in the hopeless squalor of poverty. Just below his hovel was one of three spigots which supplied water for the 45,000 people who lived lower than he. When the earth shook that night, the dirt and mud precipice that towered over their shack fell and they were swept into a hopeless darkness that threatened to extinguish their battered souls.

All the rhetoric about land reform had missed them. He had to steal to eat. His mother sold chickens from a basket on her head, walking miles each day on bare feet swollen by the filth of poverty. The veins of her legs bursting, her hope was very faint when the earth shook. She would later recall that she thought it was the end of the world and that Jesus had come to take her out of her misery. Her thoughts were only for her wayward son and invalid daughter. Clutching them with withered hands, she waited out the 35 seconds that would determine their futures.

Dr. Coca Mazariegos lived high in the mountains. His clinic was open to all. He had been the target of the communists because he was a native Mayan, he had an education, he had influence through medicine and he had married an American missionary. He was living proof that there is hope for the multitudes and it does not come from the type of armed mob that held us in the Aceh police station.

Those who would control the multitudes do so through false hopes and force. Threats and bitter words are their lives. Hatred pours out of their hearts. Usually they are people who have suffered some personal affront at the hands of the people they now hate enough to kill. Couching their hatred in lofty rhetoric, claiming some sort of divine mandate, or just cause, they incite the multitudes to take action. That action will be to intimidate or annihilate those whose message of hope is true.

The multitudes have to decide which offer is theirs. They have to find a point of connectedness to the one offering them hope. Jesus healed the sick, cleansed the leper, multiplied the loaves and fishes, and great multitudes followed Him. He gained enough influence that He had to be killed or those who controlled the public safety would lose their positions. He won the affection of the people through meeting their needs.

It is the decision of the multitudes that will determine the outcome of the nation. Mao preached a common hatred of the landed gentry. The people rose up, the landowners fled or were killed and the land became barren and unfruitful. The thought of a farmers' uprising became the great fear behind the Great Wall. When the farmers began to gather at the train station in support of the students in the Tiananmen uprising, the army had to be called in to restore public safety. The message of hatred of those who hold power had been so well learned that the new power brokers were in danger.

Preachers of such hatred had begun in Guatemala. The multitudes of the Catholic nation were hearing a theology of social and political activism as priests from France and Spain came to stir them on against their fellow Catholics who held financial and political power. The Army of the Poor funded from overseas interests and armed by night flights from Cuba were training in the mountains near Coca Mazariegos' home.

Youth by the hundreds were being offered big money to kidnap and kill executives and landholders. Private armies were being formed and every Mercedes or BMW that drove through town was in the escort of a multi-passenger vehicle whose darkened windows prevented onlookers a glimpse of the armory contained. Recruitment was strong for these youth. They would be the masses seen in demonstrations with strategically positioned student leaders in their midst ready to turn up the vehemence on a signal from the leaders. They had been recruited and trained, and then the earth shook.

Having green eyes was going to be a problem. The remote village where Lacho lay was a weapons storage facility for the Army of the Poor. The Mayen family had been landowners there for generations. Soon they would be forced to leave their lands in the peasant uprising planned for 1976. By mid-year, the unrest would build to overflow in the capital and youth from the city would come through the Motagua valley to resupply.

Sympathizers in the small villages were ready to receive and supply those who would create constant unrest in those areas around the north and east of the city until the government had fallen and the land would be theirs. Green eyes would mean that you were of the landowner's class and would need to be suppressed by the multitudes. Nothing personal, they would just circle your house and ask you to come out to a hopeless future. If you did not, they would just throw the rocks and bottles and some fire until you decided to respect them. It was the same in China, the same in Vietnam, the same in Warsaw, the same in Indonesia. And then, the earth shook.

When the dust cleared on February 4, 1976, the hopes of the revolutionaries had been destroyed. What would rebuild this nation? What possible hope were frustrated fanatics in the face of real human suffering? What words would explain how Coca, Lacho, and Hector had all been shaken and spared? How do you mobilize a mob to surround a nation and cry out that an earthquake is partial in its destruction?

Natural phenomena create multitudes, and on that cool morning a sad nation gathered its dead and began to mourn. For a moment they were hopeless and then help began to flow in from the northern nation they were learning to despise. By noon a reconstruction effort was mobilized by a Canadian and an American who had been sent to Guatemala months in advance of the event. How did they know?

Army hospitals and medicines were flown into remote areas by mission pilots and men like Coca worked for days to help the injured. Youth from the ghettos were mobilized by local churches to use their strength to get piles of rubble moved in the hope of rescuing thousands hanging from a time-line of dehydration and blood loss. Such a group dug Lacho out of his house and helped the dazed old man to find shelter.

Thousands of people came from other nations to aid in the needs of these unfortunates whose world was suddenly shaken. Without any political agenda millions of dollars flowed into the ravaged country. Hope came on love's wings.

We were invited to rebuild a village. One hundred and fifty families had their tile roofs come down on their heads. Just a few miles from the epicenter, the earth had been split in several of the fissures of the water supply and there was no longer potable water for the population. The morning the American and Canadian asked if our team would serve El Fiscal we stood on a low ridge overlooking the devastation. The medical people had been through it. We could see the multitude looking up to us to find hope. We agreed to do it and, with prayer, launched on an adventure that brought the three, Lacho, Hector, and Coca together to create hope where hope was lost.

Our first task was to register the people; Mayen, green eyes; Reyes, brown eyes; Rios, green eyes and so forth. Before a week was out we knew the racial divisions of this small population. We were most fortunate that our forms left no opportunity to register political or church affiliation. The earthquake had been impartial and so were we.

Juan Reyes was the mayor of the town. He presented a list of 150 families who needed temporary shelter and water as well as food and clothing. When Hector began to confirm the list he found that they were all youth who had been in the recruitment for Lacho's village. They were common in age and in the rubble of their homes we found materials designed to incite this mob to violence against their neighbor. When we asked Juan about it, he just shrugged his shoulders and said a foreigner would never understand.

We suggested that he put his personal wars on hold until we could get his town rebuilt and decided to put him in our intensive true hope information program. He responded to love. He got honest about the needs of the people and the town was rebuilt complete with clinic, school, churches, and a beautiful water system. But greater still was the rebuilding of the relationships between the populations. The families were able to reconcile and the instigators of hatred were asked to leave as the multitude made the connection with peace. Weapons caches were returned to the government and amnesty was given to the youth. The President of the Republic extended a "bullets for beans" campaign and most of the militia in that region surrendered their arms.

Coca had it a bit more difficult in his mountain area. The region had become a stronghold for insurgency. Training facilities were concealed behind the façade of schools. Farms had become factories for heroin and cocaine which were used to pay for the arms necessary to overthrow the government. As a medical doctor, Coca closed one eye on all of this and treated the local people without partiality. This kept him and his family safe until one of the leaders of the insurgency decided he needed to pour more hate into the multitude to overcome the love that was being demonstrated to them. They were gaining real hope for a future that did not include killing their neighbors.

Dr. Coca received multiple death threats. He moved his family to the United States but remained in the mountains to serve the suffering. He treated army, local, foreign militants without partiality until a night visitor told him he had just three days to leave the nation or be killed. They pleaded with him to go in the hope that one day he would be able to return to his homeland.

I was asked to drive Coca and the things we could load in a Volkswagen bus to the safety of the United States. Not worried about Mexico, my greatest concern was the first 50 miles as the vanload of equipment, medicine, one

Guatemalan Doc, and an American would make a great catch for young gunmen. With prayer, I flew to meet him in Guatemala City.

Our plan was to leave the city at 6 pm, which would put us in his village at midnight. We would load up in two hours and leave the village, heading north. If we went through the mountains instead of the coast road, we would be in the vicinity of people he knew and had treated. If we needed to, we could stop. Of course I never planned to stop at any of their homes because that would be a death warrant for them. It was clear that Coca had never driven a VW bus through mountains, but it sounded good at the time.

We left on schedule and although the tension was palpable, we made it through to his village and loaded without incident. With a prayer and tears we headed north out of the village to the mountain road. With each blind curve and switchback we expected to be stopped by a falling tree or a squad of gunmen.

By 2 am we had reached the main highway which is a two-lane ribbon of asphalt winding its way through volcano peaks. Tourists love to come and ride the slow chicken buses that take all day to wind their colorful way from village to village. We were not there for the scenery. The road was in really bad shape because of the earthquake, but the bus was new and amazingly powerful, for a late-seventies VW.

We passed Coca's birth village at dawn and he openly wondered if he would ever get back there. We had kissed his mother, father, and little sister goodbye in the capital. There was a great deal of emotion as their son, the hope of their futures, was forced from his homeland and practice. Pausing before the cathedral, we said goodbye to the town and rejoined the north road that would take us to Mexico and then the U.S.

I first saw the pick-up truck in my right-side mirror. He was swerving from lane to lane with each curve. As fear gripped my heart I hoped it was just a drunk farmer on his way home. We came to a straight part of the road and, just as we reached the next bend I got a good look at him. It was a white Ford, about a '73, and it had wooden rails on the back. It was the kind we use on farms to haul cattle. This morning the cargo was a group of weapon-wielding youth. Their rifle barrels were pointed into the air, but there was no doubt of their intent. Accelerating into the coming left curve I told Coca that something was about to happen.

We took the curve to the inside and, as I straightened out for the bottom, I saw the trap designed to capture us. There was an old Mercedes on the right side of the road and a multi-passenger blocking the left lane. We were expected to respond to their hand motions to stop and pull behind the Mercedes.

"Coca, get down on the floor," I shouted and pushed him down. He knelt there praying for the Lord to get us through this.

Slowing, as if to stop, and making eye contact with the man on the road I noticed that the drivers were out of both cars. Terror is so used to its strength that it sometimes fails to account for the few of us who really do not care if we die because we have a greater hope. Their hold is only good if we have hope only in this life.

"Stay down," I said as I calmly slowed and looked in the mirror to see if the chase truck had caught up to me. I have no idea why, but he was not there.

Down-shifting and fixing a stare in the eyes of the man on my side of the car, I let out the clutch and accelerated through the situation. We just cleared the Mercedes and, at about 50 miles per hour, caught the gear with ease and sped on toward Mexico. The next three hours were a study in hope. With every curve we expected gunfire, until we reached the international zone. Exhilarated by hope realized, we drove straight through Mexico and the United States until we reached the northern state in which Coca, rejoined with his family, restarted his life.

The earthquake shaped these three lives and millions more. It broke the back of the beast of communism. Youth have grown with education. While there is crime, there are no more truckloads of militant youth searching to kidnap and hold for ransom innocents given only to help the multitudes. To be sure, there is political activity; but now the nation enjoys the peaceful transfer of power as all parties work together for the good of the multitude.

***

As we sat in our Indonesian cell I thought about the fear that day. The threats, the mobs, the violence came back as, through the distance, I heard again the sound of the hate-filled mob outside our barred windows. The Banker held up six fingers and I settled in to think some more.

CHAPTER FOURTEEN

A bright sunny day

IT was a bright sunny day in Ulan Bator. We had been five days on the train and it had finally stopped. Anyone who says it is a small world has never ridden the rails from Hong Kong to London. It is not a small world.

Our group of five was tired of being on a train. Eager to stretch our legs, we asked the conductor at what time the train would leave. He responded in German saying "Fier" and holding up four fingers. Released for a few hours we quickly grabbed some things, and strode across the platform and into the sleepy town of Ulan Bator. Capital of the Soviet republic of Mongolia, this 1985 whistle-stop town had been the crossroads of two great cultures.

We walked through streets nearly empty of people. The buildings were primitive compared to the splendor of Beijing. We had passed the corral areas of the nomadic herds and a junkyard filled with rusting Russian military hardware. Now we wanted to get some fresh bread, maybe some meat of some kind and make it back to the train for our journey to Siberia.

At each shop we were greeted with such warmth we forgot to keep track of time. Handshake by handshake we made new friends. The Mongolian people were very receptive to our attempts at communication. We found steaming bread and cakes and were having a great time. We went from building to building shaking hands with the people and taking pictures with them. Glancing at the watch we calculated that we had about half an hour before we had to be back at the train.

After a few more handshakes, we walked quickly to the platform. There was no train in sight. None at all. A complete International Train had disappeared. Approaching a guard I asked with hand gestures, "Where is the train?"

Also using hand gestures he said, "Gone."

With my hands I asked, "Gone?"

"Da" he said.

"I held out my hands in the way you would receive hand cuffs and said, "Take us away."

Laughingly he took us to the train station and went off to find someone who could speak English. After an appropriate round of clarification, blame placing, and apology we settled into the adventure. We waited to see what would happen.

Two of us were loaded into a car and taken "down town." There we were questioned by a matronly Mongolian lady who turned out to be very important. She explained that we had returned late for the train but, not to worry, they had advised the Russians, and our things would be removed from the train when it reached the border. Now, as to ongoing arrangements, she wanted to know if we had any money. We had little between us because we had left everything on the train. She was amused to find that included our passports and travel documents. We were literally people without names or countries. She promised that she would take good care of us.

We were taken back to the train station and allowed to rest in a room with no door handle on the inside. It was very clean and neat and we were very comfortable. We spoke little, but were not unhappy, feeling at no time as if we were at risk.

At about six in the evening we were ushered to a train. It was another of the steam engine type we had ridden to this point, and as we entered our compartment under police guard, the other passengers took quick note of our "foreign" look. They were instructed to give us lots of space and obligingly closed their compartment doors.

Now we began to speak to each other concerning the dilemma we faced in the morning. Our bags were sure to be searched and they contained very valuable Bibles and cassette tapes in Mongolian and Russian. Transport of these in the numbers we had could only mean that we were smuggling them across the Soviet Border. We were headed into a certain international situation. As team leader, it was my job to figure this out.

I was really hungry. The bread we had bought was gone and I had to think, which is always easier with food. I tried to find a dining car but was told there was not one on this train. It seemed that everyone on the train was in uniform. We found out through a student who spoke some English that this was a military train returning troops from the war in Afghanistan. With that news I decided to stay in the compartment.

One of our team had a hunger disorder. He had to eat every six hours or he got really grumpy. I chose the corridor rather than the complaining. Standing very alone at a window, I reflected on our situation. We were on a Russian military train going toward the Siberian border. Ahead of us, the police certainly had our passports, money, and enough evidence to put us in any jail. We did not have food or water and the night was going to be very tense with the attitudes in the group. Things did not look good.

"Deutch?" The question startled me.

"Nyet Deutch," I responded without thinking, "Amerikanski."

"Amerikanski!" The voice roared back.

The hand was big enough to cover both my shoulders. I looked up and to my left into the smiling face of the largest white man I have ever seen. In one move he swept me down the hall and into his compartment. There, five other men in uniform were enjoying black bread and fat back sandwiches with brown mustard and vodka. The sight brought back wonderful childhood memories. When times were very bad, we would take a strip of pork fat, put it on wheat bread and spread the warmth of hot mustard over it. Filling, and filled with the energy we needed in the freezing winters, there could have been no better meal to ward off the cold Gobi night. They were Russian military and celebrating going home.

"Amerikanski," he announced as they made a place for me to sit. He ducked back out into the corridor and soon brought the rest of our group. To their offer of vodka I informed them of our Christian faith and they very respectfully changed to black tea.

The train sped through the night as we shared our lives. We talked of Cuba, two of the men had been there as technicians, and of the war in Afghanistan. I was embarrassed to realize I was unaware of this struggle. We talked about missiles and nuclear weapons. We talked about our countries being enemies. We were very frank and cordial. They had always wanted to tell Americans how they felt about things. They also wanted to hear how Americans felt about Russia.

We began to exchange songs. They sang military and folk songs and we sang worship songs. As we alternated, we tried to learn each other's languages. We were thrilled to see them sing "Hallelujah" and raise their hands as we had. The night was filled with love for each other. We, who were cast in the role of enemies, would for one night be friends in the common bond of food and song shared.

Our host gave the word and we were returned to our cabin. Stomachs full and hearts overflowing we settled in for a deep sleep. The enemy had become our friend and we had hope for the morning.

Dawn brought us to the platform on the Mongolian side of the border. We were ushered from the train to certain trouble. We watched for our singing companions but they were nowhere to be seen. There in the police department of the train station were our things. Each bag had been emptied and inventoried. The currency was laid out one bill at a time and the serial numbers of each bill was recorded. The tapes and Bibles were also inventoried, and in very neat piles. The chief, another matronly lady asked us to verify all of the contents and sign for them. We thanked her for her thorough care of us and she allowed us to repack our things while she stepped to her office. Upon completing the packing we were invited for tea with her, at which time she asked me to sign a letter. I was provided with an English copy, signed both and returned them to her.

The letter verified that we had been well treated and that all possessions had been returned with nothing missing. She was emphatic to state that we were guests in her country. She could not vouch for the Russians, but Mongolia was a friend of the United States.

We were amazed, and delighted at her attitude and with thanks took on the challenge of getting all this stuff into Russia. Customs was a breeze as was immigration. We were greeted with friendly smiles everywhere. These were supposed to be our enemies. Every one of us had been raised with the thought of having to run to a bomb shelter when the ballistic missiles brought their payload of death to us. For enemies, they were very friendly.

***

As I sat in this cell, thinking about the youth in the street, I remembered that big Russian officer. He was trained for warfare against us. I had been trained for warfare against him. He had grown up thinking that I would bomb him and his family to become richer. I had been raised to think that he would nuke me and my family to take the whole world. We had been made enemies by those who taught us.

What about these young people? Who was teaching them? Jesus said to love our enemies, but today we never get the chance to meet them. I decided as the day wore on that, given the opportunity to meet some of these people, I would at least be friendly about it.

Maybe Leck was right. Maybe it was just an honor in the sight of the Lord to show forgiveness in the face of persecution. Why did I think of them as the enemy? Who had first said they were? Where did I get that idea?

My reverie was once again interrupted. Interpol was back.

"I Send You"

Matthew 10:2-4

[2]*Now the names of the twelve apostles are these: first, Simon, who is called Peter, and Andrew his brother; James the son of Zebedee, and John his brother;* [3]*Philip and Bartholomew; Thomas and Matthew the tax collector; James the son of Alphaeus, and Lebbaeus, whose surname was Thaddaeus;* [4]*Simon the Cananite, and Judas Iscariot, who also betrayed Him.*

2 Corinthians 11:22-29

[22]*Are they Hebrews? So am I. Are they Israelites? So am I. Are they the seed of Abraham? So am I.* [23]*Are they ministers of Christ?--I speak as a fool--I am more: in labors more abundant, in stripes above measure, in prisons more frequently, in deaths often.* [24]*From the Jews five times I received forty stripes minus one.* [25]*Three times I was beaten with rods; once I was stoned; three times I was shipwrecked; a night and a day I have been in the deep;* [26]*in journeys often, in perils of waters, in perils of robbers, in perils of my own countrymen, in perils of the Gentiles, in perils in the city, in perils in the wilderness, in perils in the sea, in perils among false brethren;* [27]*in weariness and toil, in sleeplessness often, in hunger and thirst, in fastings often, in cold and nakedness--* [28]*besides the other things, what comes upon me daily: my deep concern for all the churches.* [29]*Who is weak, and I am not weak? Who is made to stumble, and I do not burn with indignation?*

CHAPTER FIFTEEN

The Hindu Kush

"Mr. Mark," he was very professional. "We are now satisfied that you had no idea what was happening here today. We see that you have just happened to be in the wrong place at the wrong time. This is an innocent mistake. We are sorry for the difficulty you are having and are talking with the leaders of the group to allow you to leave. Please be assured that we are doing everything we can to ensure your safety."

I not only had no idea why an Interpol policeman was at a sleepy little town, why a Moslem radical was stuffed into an "I love America" T-shirt and ball cap, or why a helicopter was sent for tourists, or why anyone would bring a surface-to-air weapon to a religious rally, I also had no idea why a "Ninja" was negotiating for peace or a squad of commandoes was on its way to the scene. But, it looked pretty interesting from where I sat.

Until that day the Chinese had set the record for making things appear other than they were. This group was pressing for the record. With more questions than answers and time passing without direct pressure, I sat back to remember other pressure-packed days in my life.

✳✳✳

JUST a few years before, we had decided to cross the Hindu Kush, that passage between Pakistan and Afghanistan that is so contested today. We assembled our team in Singapore and flew to Islamabad. From there we got tickets for buses that would take us over the 17,000-foot pass and into China. It was the route of Marco Polo, one of the ancient silk roads. We were carrying several thousand copies of the Gospel of Luke and the Book of Acts in the Uygher language. This Arabic people are thought by some to be one of the lost tribes of Israel and by others to be a displaced people group. They inhabit the desert strip of oil-rich land between China and the Moslem nations.

The ascent was wonderful, the Indus River providing a spectacular opportunity to ride the cable boxes that are the only link to many mountain villages. Passing K-2 and glacier flows we saw many things I never dreamed existed.

We ate the same style noodles and pizza that inspired Polo to take the trade back to Italy. The team was fun, everyone getting along fine even with the altitude sickness and travel stress. Finally, we crossed the peak and wound our way down through sand dunes and rock faces to the border control at the Chinese city of Tashgergens.

It was here that we ran into a difficulty. Ambition had conquered reason and my son and I stood with 15 bags at our feet and the tour group on the other side of customs. No one takes 15 bags for a bus trip through the desert. Of course the customs officials wanted to know what was in the bags and, of course, when they found the books, they wanted to have an in-depth interview with us. Dispatching the rest of the group to a hotel in a neighboring town, they invited my son, Sammy, and me to a private interview.

Escorted to a modern office building we were introduced to the Chief of Customs who allowed us to rest in the hallway for about two hours while he and his team made a thorough inventory of the contents of our bags. A sparrow flew into the hall while we were there. He flew from side to side and in and out through the window. Though captive, he was free. Though free, he was captive. I watched him for some time thinking of the old hymn, "His eye is on the sparrow…"

The Customs Chief returned from the search and inventory and invited us into his office. A Uygher national, as opposed to a Han Chinese, he was very interested in why we had brought the Jesus film and books in his language and not in Chinese.

"Some friends asked us to carry them since we were coming this way," I offered.

The answer was completely true. I had no idea of a delivery plan or any contacts or any such thing. It was not my plan and they were not my books.

He asserted that he was Uygher and thanked us for our interest in his people. We were released to the Chinese police who were very nice once we sorted out the fact that they had separated me from my son, and that, unless I was officially arrested and charged, they were not supposed to do so. They brushed the complaint aside and turned us over to the Chinese Border Police who recorded our data and took us to the rest of the group.

We heard from them that they had been questioned individually and that only our other son, Matt, had been given a real shake down. He was frightened and I could see that all of our efforts over the years of making the Chinese our "friends" and not our "enemies," were going to perish if something positive did not soon occur.

We traveled the next day to the ancient city of Kashgar. What a place to see. From the ancient Mosque to the horse market at the bazaar, ancient cultures of East and West blend in a display of color and tradition. We enjoyed walking all day and praying for the people. We were warmly received by the Head Imam of the mosque who asked if we had brought the New Testament. He had been listening to Far East Broadcasting and wanted desperately to have a New Testament. One was found for him and we delightedly pushed on.

The following morning came the knock at the door and the phrase we love to hate, "Mr. Mark, could you come with us please?"

As we walked down the hall to the questioning room I kept telling myself, "I love these guys. They are just doing their job. There is nothing personal about this. They are nice people."

Sam called out from behind me, "If they throw us out we are flying. We do not want to go out by bus or train."

"Mr. Mark, I have to inform you that you are under arrest. The nature of the charge against you is a threat to the national security of the People's Republic of China. This is a very serious offense. The punishment can be very serious. Please cooperate with us fully and give honest answers to our questions." He was serious.

The room was like a movie set. There was one wooden chair under a single light bulb, two policemen smoking and blowing smoke in my face, the "nice guy" trying to "help me" through the situation while going through my personal effects. The three were very difficult to love, they were rapidly becoming enemies.

They had chosen my Bible and passport as the items that would affect me most. The English speaker started taking papers from my Bible and asking me about each one. They were bulletins of past services in different churches. A photo of a kid we were trying to pray off drugs and the like. I watched the way he handled the book. There was no respect given to the Word of God. Not personally offended, I tucked the thought away as a later preaching point.

Jesus told the disciples, "Do not worry when you are arrested. Take no thought for what you are going to say. The Holy Spirit will put the words in your mouth."

I relaxed and watched the scene play out.

"You are in really big trouble. A threat to national security is like a spy charge. I would suggest you tell us exactly why you have come here." His sincerity was mind boggling.

"I am a threat to your national security?" I was equally sincere.

"Would you please tell me how a middle-aged fat man who does not even speak Chinese can be a threat to the national security of the world's largest nation?" It was a good question and I enjoyed asking it.

"You are a Christian, right?" he asked.

"Of course I am, everyone should be," I responded.

"That is a threat to our national security," he explained, as if I should understand.

"How is my personal faith a threat to your national security?" I asked, honestly dumbfounded over his reply.

"Everywhere you go you will tell people about Jesus, right?" He smiled.

"Of course, sharing is like breathing for a Christian," I answered.

"That is a threat to our national security." He nodded to the other two as though they should agree. They nodded affirmatively.

"How is that a threat to your national security?" I offered.

"If they hear, they will believe." He leaned forward and our eyes met. I looked for some sense of light in this man's eyes. He was quoting the scripture Paul wrote and which we all know as the reason to go. I saw no light in the eyes.

"If they believe, we cannot control them." He was very serious now; we were nose to nose.

"You people will not be able to do in China what you did in Europe!" His emphatic declaration led me to the next question.

"What did we people do in Europe?" I was now sincere to hear his rehearsed point of view.

"Communism will not fall in China! You Christians will not take us over. You are a threat to our national security." He began to roughly thumb through the pages of my Bible for effect. I thought he would throw it at me, but he regained control and sat down again.

"Please give me my Bible," I asked with respect.

"Oh, you want this book?" he said, holding it back the way one would tease a child. "What is so special about this book?"

Ask Jonas Salk about the Polio vaccine. Ask Bill Gates about software. Ask NASA about space travel.

"Let me tell you, son. That is the last thing I touch before I sleep. It is the first thing I reach for when I awaken. It is the book that changed my life. It is the book that saved me from hell. It is mine and I will ask you to give it to me." Eyes locked, hearts aflame, we faced each other. He shrugged and handed me the book.

The next morning we were escorted to the police station, finger-printed, documented, passports stamped to exit sooner than planned. We indeed went by bus and train for more than a week with police escort. They were very concerned about who we would see, and what we would say. In every hotel in which we stayed they briefed the staff concerning us.

We had daily opportunity to share the hope that was in us. Actually, the briefings served to arouse hunger in the hotel staff and management. They wanted to know about a faith so precious we were ready to risk all for it.

When we boarded the flight from Xian to depart China, a policeman came on board and the flight attendants asked everyone to produce their documents for him. From my seat in row 17 I called out, "Are you looking for Mr. Mark?"

Affirming that he was, he motioned for me to come forward. I did, and after a close inspection of my passport, he bid me a safe journey and exited the plane. I turned in the aisle to face a plane full of very nervous people.

"You are probably asking yourselves, 'What did he do?'"

"I am guilty of preaching Christ in China. This is the state of Christianity in China. The believer here is seen as a threat to National Security because he has found hope in Jesus. For this message we are being asked to leave China today. It is our joy to fly with you all."

Returning to my seat, I received the applause of the other passengers and the best in-flight service we have ever known.

A year later I was in Long Island, New York, to participate in a Missions Conference. One of the speakers worked in that region of China and asked if we could speak. With only the Pastor present, he said, "Sorry if they gave you a rough time last year."

"What?" I asked, surprised that he knew.

"Yes, it was all arranged. We felt that you would have the maturity to pull it off. The bags that were confiscated were delivered in the region. Thank you very much."

✳✳✳

Who is the enemy? It wasn't this brother and it wasn't the police. It wasn't the kids in the Aceh heat and it wasn't even the Irate Imam. The enemy is the one who is trying to keep people from knowing the truth that will set them free.

Through the demonstration of love and patience, we have seen the worst situations turned for good. As we stood at level six, I gained strength from what we have come to call, "The China Experience."

CHAPTER SIXTEEN

They were back

They were back. The "Ninja", the "Interpol," and the "Uniform" stood at our doorway about to give us the hourly update. As the afternoon had worn on it became clear that negotiation was not going to win the day and at some point a real show of force was going to happen. How that would all work out, was their part to play. Ours was to be the sincerely sorry lot who happened to be in the wrong place at the wrong time.

Four hours had passed since the Irate Imam had shouted through the window. Several events had occurred. The mob had fallen into a pattern of attacking the building four times in an hour. They had succeeded in burning our car and the police chief's car. They had gained entrance to the building twice, had broken out the windows, and had set fires in the front offices. They had rejected all offers of negotiation, wanting only for us to be handed over to them.

I had a couple of questions: like, why they hadn't just pointed the surface-to-air at us and blown the front off the building, but thought it better to just listen. The Banker had seven fingers up when I looked over. I felt a bit nervous. The Doctor's vein was up again and the Chinese had that look they get when they are about to take on the whole mob single-handedly. This was a good time for a quiet confident leadership style made possible by the presence of the Lord and a solid history of steps to this point. It is true that today's pressure is preparing us for future victories.

Back to the report, it was going to be dark soon. That was bad news unless the commandos made it before nightfall. They felt there was no way they could defend this small building in the night, so when the army arrived, there would be a lot of shouting and shooting and we should stay low and be ready to do what we were told.

Looking beyond them I saw the arms locker open and the orange-taped banana clips issued to the police. They looked tired and very nervous. Some glanced at me with disdain, others with indifference. I shall forever appreciate the professionalism of the Indonesian police.

Sit tight. Stay away from windows. Do not try to escape on your own. Help is coming. We will get out of here. Rounds were fired in the front and away they went to their duty stations.

I looked at the Banker and was not reassured by his smile, the eighth finger was up.

Whose plan had this been? It was a fair question and had a team member asked it I would have taken responsibility to prevent any division at this time of pressure. Thank God the men on our team were mature enough to not ask it aloud although we could see in each other's eyes the question, "Are we here in the will of God?"

Returning to my waiting seat I pondered the conflicting doctrines. One says, "If you are in the will of God, everything is wonderful and goes well."

The other says, "If you are in the will of God, you will suffer in this life."

The real question is, "Who got you into this, or did you do it yourself?"

Four events in my life have caused me to assess that question, "Who sent you here?" It is most often asked by someone who has *decided that I do not have the cunning, or appear to have the intellect or spiritual power to be in the place I am. Or... in the case of the Interpol, to be so uninformed or stupid.*

✳✳✳

ONE morning my phone rang in the small office in Pennsylvania. My secretary said that Lester Summerall was on the line. Dr. Summerall was a hero of mine. As the founder and president of the Lester Summerall Evangelist Association he was a pathfinder for those of us who desired to take the message of healing and deliverance to the nations. I was shocked that he had called me.

"Are you brother Geppert?" Rough from preaching, his voice commanded respect.

"Yes sir, I am." I hoped I didn't sound too young to him.

"I hope I didn't interrupt anything important?" He was polite and powerful.

"No, sir, glad to take the call." Actually thrilled would have been a better word.

"May I ask you a few questions?" He was very polite.

"Sure, anything." I was very interested to know how he heard about me and what he wanted.

For the next 15 to 20 minutes he asked about people, places, and things where I had been. He had heard of arrests, of the nations touched and of my involvement with television in Pittsburgh. He knew we took Bibles to nations. He knew we had begun in Latin America. I never found out how he knew. He was used to asking the questions.

He made the arrangements for my wife and me to visit at their TV studios in Indiana. These included a lovely hotel, breakfast and lunch before our return to Pittsburgh.

In everything he was a gentlemen and an example of a supportive older minister guiding the younger man.

He and his wife invited us to a time of prayer during which they placed their hands over our heads and commissioned us to the calling the Lord had placed in our lives. I understand that he had been commissioned the same way by Smith Wigglesworth who had received the same commissioning by George Mueller. Such a thing has often kept my mind in times like Aceh.

The inevitable question we face in the Apostolic or "sent one" ministry is, "Who sent you?"

We obviously cannot lay hands on ourselves as Robert Duval did in the movie, "The Apostle." We cannot be self-motivated and properly represent the Lord among the nations. But, there is no doubt that there is, in the body of Christ, a place for those who carry on the mission of the "Sent Ones."

This was Dr. Summerall's question and it would surely be that of the Interpol and Indonesian police once our situation ended.

"Who sent you?" This is the question that takes the disciple out of the realm of self-motivation, dutiful service, and expected activity, the realm of "what you do" and into the realm of "whose authority is behind you."

Like the young teacher in Nepal or the Guatemalan who finds his self worth, the disciple will often get a picture of truth and run with it as fast as he can. He will preach till he drops, pray till heaven answers, give till he starves, and then look for more to do. This commitment level was typified by Peter when he said during his 18 months as a disciple, "Not just my hands and feet, but all of me."

When Jesus was going to send Peter He corrected this mindset with the words, "When you were young you went where you wanted and did what you wanted to do. When you are mature another will bind you hand and foot and take you where you would not go."

This scripture found in John 21, is the essence of the ministry of those sent ones. Toward the end of the disciple phase of maturity they realize that as Dr. Costa Dier told me, "Your life is not your own. First you belong to Jesus, He bought you. Then you belong to your family, they love you. Then you belong to the church, they sustain you. Then you belong to the nations, they wait for you."

Those in the "Sent Ones" ministry preserve these four close relationships. They will die for Christ. For them, "to live is Christ and to die is gain." It was this thought that gave us hope no matter what the Aceh outcome.

They love their families. A study of the children of "sent ones" will find them heading corporations, leading in the health and education professions, stable in marriage and guiding the coming generations.

They are sustained by the church. "Sent ones" do not have time to sustain themselves financially. The symbiotic relationship they have with local churches releases spiritual, human, and material resources for both.

The nations wait for them. The police in every land want to know the truth of authority without corruption. Authority is ordained by God to serve those who walk in His ways. In a later chapter of this book you will hear of a man who waited a lifetime to meet someone who was raised in a Christian home.

Dr. Summerall and Dr. Dier were more than familiar with the admonition to let no one call you an "Apostle." They held to the better phrase, "sent one." And they were both fully conversant in the principles involved.

Being a "sent one" is very simple. A nation has a need. You are made aware of that need. A church receives an offering for that need. You deliver the offering to the point of need. As you travel you become aware of the opportunities to demonstrate the love of Jesus through meeting needs. You report to the church the opportunity to meet a need and glorify the Lord in the process. They pray about it and when the Lord confirms the need and His desire to meet it, He leads them to get in touch with you and you are sent by them to meet the need. Actually, the ministry of a "sent one" is extremely simple compared to that of a Pastor. A Pastor has to look after the flock, know their names, and minister to their needs.

A "sent one" just goes out and demonstrates the love of Jesus to those who are waiting for him to come. Sometimes they are waiting with mobs in the streets, but that is all part of being a "sent one."

And what is the difference between a "sent one" and an "evangelist?"

The "sent one" is a rock upon which the church can be built. He has the ability to organize, administer, and deliver physical answers to needs. The evangelist can proclaim the message with signs and wonders, break through in difficult places, demonstrate the power of God in the miraculous. The "sent one" can do all of these things and leave an indigenous structure behind. "Upon this rock I will build my church…"

✳✳✳

So, these are the things on which a "sent one" reflects as the sun sets for what may be the last time on his life. Have I run the race? Have I fought the fight? Have I completed my "course"? As I sat there in Aceh the resounding answer in my spirit was, "Yes, you can come home now."

The peace that touched my soul in that moment was like nothing I have ever felt before or since. I was ready to be face to face with Jesus. The feeling grew as I walked about the small space. It was a very peaceful light feeling. I looked in the faces of my friends and thought I saw a bit of it there. Beyond human resolve, it was the promised preparation of the Holy Spirit.

The call

IVANA Madzur had taken the step. She was being sent to Berlin. She loved the Lord. She loved her mother and father. In my last dinner with them we celebrated that love into the evening as very proud parents talked of the wonderful young woman who was their daughter. Her church was sending her. They affirmed her call and her gifts and though she was young in age, she was not in experience. They were excited to send her.

A nation was calling. In fact, many nations were calling. Actually, the whole world was calling for relief for the lie of atheism. People behind the Iron and Bamboo curtains knew there was a God and that the state was not it. Their cry reached her heart and God gave her the calling to respond. She was not the only one of their fellowship who hungered for the deliverance of the nations. Her priest, Roman Trichynski, cried out night and day for the deliverance of Poland.

Our meeting was a classic case of "Who sent you?"

Leaving the "J" bus at route's end we alighted to find her waiting for us. It was late afternoon and we were about to meet the young man selected to restore spirituality to the Solidarity Movement. Jerzy Popieluszko, the spiritual father of solidarity had been martyred the year before. His body, wrapped with chains and dumped into the Warsaw River had floated to the surface and been found by farmers several kilometers south of Warsaw. The movement had become political under the leadership of Lech Walesa and the church was concerned with the secular direction it was taking.

The bishops had met and determined that a young man who was involved with the youth movement was the one who should become Jerzy Popieluszko's replacement. He was sharp. He was respected. He was Charismatic. He had the heart of the coming generation. The movement had a martyr, what it needed was another "sent one."

We entered the vine-covered prayer grotto and there far ahead stood a solitary figure in European cassock. Black robes from shoulder to gravel, he was the embodiment of what the Russians feared. This man stood still with authority.

As we came closer Ivana could hardly contain herself. "I know it is the will of God for you two to meet," she proclaimed wringing her young hands in delight. "I just know it is supposed to happen."

Roman greeted us with enthusiasm. Looking deeply into my eyes he said, "You are the one."

Taken back I asked Ivana, "What does he mean 'I am the one.'"

Not needing the translator he again said, "You are the one I have seen."

Their community had been fasting and praying for a messenger to come, sent by the Lord to answer a very difficult question for the young people. As Catholics their only example of full-time service was a priest or a nun. The youth wanted to know if you could be married, serve

God, and have a family. They wanted to meet someone who served the Lord and had a family. If so, they would continue in Solidarity. If not, they had some serious reservations about how far they could continue in the movement.

"You are the one I saw in the dream." Roman verified every feature from my eyes to my Levis. "You are the sent one."

We talked that night about another visit. One of 23 days in which I would be accompanied by a Charismatic Catholic Priest who would affirm to them the message I would bring. I was sure Father Mike Silvagna would come. He loved the Lord, was filled with the Holy Spirit, and would certainly be sent by his community. We planned more than 50 meetings with youth and the final Eucharist with the Bishop of the Pope's home church. Little did we know at the time, the Lord had even more in store. We sang through the night and I listened to their stories of life under the Russians.

These communist atheists couched their natural hatred of the Poles in political and spiritual phrases. When cornered on economy, they persecuted the church. When their unproductive state-run factories could not meet quotas, they made life more difficult for the Poles. The state police were brutal and often the church had to meet in the forests. Ivana was one of those the Lord had raised up and the visitors who rode the rails were the lifeline for materials. They needed a prayer curriculum for the nations. Something that was simply Biblical. I suggested the *Change the World School of Prayer* by Dick Eastman and they asked me to bring Dick with me when I came. Knowing that Dick is a "sent one" it was not difficult to say, "Yes."

With hugs all around we set the time for the following spring and asked the Lord to bring it to pass.

I returned to the States to make arrangements. Mike was easy. He would be sent out by his community as I had thought. We had to clear schedule for Dick, but he was able to be sent by his ministry combining the Poland stop with a trip to Rumania. We settled the plans and I headed once again for China and the Trans-Siberian.

This trip went off very well and I arrived in Kiev with the blossoming of the tulips. Spring is beautiful on the Dnieper River and Kiev was in full bloom. I visited the tomb of St. Andrew, another "sent one" who had come from Jerusalem after Pentecost and had brought the good news of Jesus to those in this valley and beyond. Spending a day of prayer in his burial place renewed my sense of the irresistible force of the multitude that now traveled all the earth proclaiming the hope they had found in Jesus.

While I was sitting in the cathedral a group of tourists were ushered in. The tour guide sat next to me and decided to try out some English. "Do you like the relics?" he asked.

"Yes," I replied. "Do you know who this man was?"

"He was some early Christian during that era," the young man offered. "We no longer believe in such things. But the building is nice and the architecture unique to the former period." He looked at me as if begging for a rebuttal.

"Not everyone has stopped believing," I said gently. "There are some yellow tulips among the reds."

"But, there were not many," he answered and, with a wry smile, returned to his group.

I had no money in Kiev. Another conflict of "everything goes easy when you are in the will of God" and "those who serve shall suffer need." The actual fact was I had never had money on the trip and the two brothers with whom I had traveled through China and Russia had needed all the money to get to London. Dick and Mike were bringing me some money from our sending church, so it was just a couple of days before I would have regular meals again. There were no meals served in Aceh either.

The next day I prayed all day. At noon there was a power surge and the chimes and song of the revolution failed to play in Kiev. I felt the Lord saying to get on a train and get out of town. Stopping at the hotel travel desk I asked if I could leave that night. They were very happy to accommodate me and within an hour I was on a train for Poland.

Sent off by the driver, I arrived to a train packed with young people. They had bread and cheese. Stomach full, I slept to the rhythm of the rails and prepared my thoughts for the coming three weeks in Poland. Little did I know that the morning's events would change the world.

We were delayed crossing into Poland. Not a problem, I watched a very interesting program on nuclear safety and wondered at the Russians' openness about their nuclear energy program. All along the railway we had seen reactors and super power plants. It was reassuring to see so much TV time given to safety. Especially touching were the scenes of children playing in the shadow of the cooling towers. Perfectly safe, perfectly clean, they were the pride of Soviet achievement.

Arriving in Poland I made my way to Mr. Szymanski's house and waited for Dick to arrive. We would meet at the Forum Hotel and then I would take him out to the convent. He did not arrive the first day so I went on out and checked in with the Sisters of Saint Felix. They were very happy to have someone to take care of and I really did not mind the attention. These Charismatic Nuns were so filled with joy. Their worship was Holy Spirit filled and their service was without equal.

The next morning Ivana came out to the mother house and we all sat down to a big breakfast. I was ready for it and could hardly wait through the time of meditation and special prayers. Roman was there and Dick and Mike were coming in that day, having been delayed a day in their plans. Mother Superior came in to join us. She was carrying a tray with some kind of juice.

"Ivana," I asked. "What is that?"

"That is iodine," Ivana answered. "Mother says we have to drink it."

"Why am I going to drink iodine?" I asked.

"It's for your thyroid," Ivana scolded.

"What is wrong with my thyroid?" I responded.

"Shh, just drink it." She was emphatic.

"Father Roman," I sought help in my friend. "Do I have to drink this iodine?"

"You have not heard the news?" He turned to look straight into my face. "While you were praying in Kiev a nuclear reactor at Chernobyl exploded. We are in the middle of a cloud of radiation that can kill if it gets into your thyroid so we have been encouraged to drink the iodine to neutralize any affect of the radiation. It is up to you if you want to take it or not."

I sat there putting pieces of the puzzle together. I recalled the power surge, the urgency in my spirit to leave town, the manner of prayer in which I was involved before the surge. The danger we all were in. Dick and Mike were being sent into the cloud. It all swirled around in a kaleidoscope of colors. I poured the iodine in a plant, finished breakfast and headed for the Forum to meet Dick.

He brought magazines and newspapers from the free world. He told of the visions and dreams people had concerning his trip. He had almost called it off, but he knew that I was in the cloud and that Mike was being sent to join and he had to follow through with it. They will always be in my heart as brothers who hazarded their lives for me and for the gospel.

✳✳✳

Three others were hazarding their lives. The Doctor, the Banker, and our Chinese friend could be within minutes of eternity. I looked across the darkening space and marveled at them. They were just ordinary people. They had no claim to greatness, but they had followed the Lord. They had been sent by Him to this time and place.

I am sure the Apostles did not look like the paintings in Grand Cathedrals. In fact, if you look into their ethnicity, they were pretty common people. They had grown from hope to belief, from belief to discipline and from discipline to being sent. Having proven their faithfulness and being filled with the Holy Spirit they were compelled to go. Those two in Poland and these three with whom I shared an afternoon of adventure had one thing in common with Andrew. They went where they were sent.

The peace was there again and with it a certainty; I would be seeing Jesus soon.

CHAPTER EIGHTEEN

Who had sent them?

W HO had sent them, all these people trekking, riding the rails, walking through cities, eating pizza in the "old towns" of Europe's cities and risking international incidents? Who had sent them? Was it a big organization? Had a church sent them as missionaries? Did they have a special sense of calling or a dream, or an angelic invitation?

How did they know they were supposed to make one of these "faith journeys?" How did they get time off from work, how did their families react? How often did they go? If they got into trouble, who would take care of them? Were they all young or were some of them elderly? Did they go alone or were they always in a group?

Who sent them? Who paid for their travel? How did they know where they would stay or what they would do? Who decided what they would eat or where they would sleep? Were these "once in a lifetime" events, or did they go on a regular schedule? How much did a trip cost? How often could they go?

Who sent them? How were they trained? Did they all come from the same city? How was the itinerary decided?

As dusk slowly sapped the features from their faces, I

looked about our sanctuary and studied my three friends. The Chinese had been first with the idea. It had come about in conversations we had about Islam and its spread, and significant places where Jesus would have us pray. Firmly persuaded that the whole global issue was the depleting resource of oil and the increasing demand of urban growth, we felt together that the Moslems were trying to control field and flow, supply and demand.

Our interest was not economic, but spiritual. We noticed a pattern over 12 years; economic pressure, followed by population increase due to the Islamic allowance of four wives and many children, followed by overcrowding of land resource, followed by redistribution of property and allocation of tribal lands to urban dwellers in what National Geographic Magazine had heralded as a great accomplishment of the Suharto, Javanese, government. We had been to western, southern, central and east Sumatra; but, had not gone north to Aceh Province.

Aceh was strategic to oil flow. Aceh was home to the Exxon/Mobil Refinery. Aceh was referred to as 100% Moslem. Aceh was the last Province to join the Republic of Indonesia. It was reported that Christians in Aceh had a most difficult time. The voices that rose from recently discovered mass graves gave evidence of mutual intense hatred. The "Java Government" and the "Free Aceh" forces used the ideological struggle to fuel their uniformed or "rag tag" bands against each other. While oil was the issue, their passions of faith fueled the flames. "Free Aceh" wanted to fulfill their reputation as 100% Moslem. The Jakarta Government, located on the island of Java were sworn to uphold "Pancasila" or the "one god many paths" policy which is an abomination to the monotheistic Moslem.

He, the Chinese, had heard of the plight of Christians in Aceh and had asked if I thought we could take a drive through it, pray in major and significant places, and see if it was as reported. We had hoped to report our findings to prayer ministries for their focused intercession. We were interested only in the spiritual side, being neither businessmen nor political activists. We had traveled through many countries in our endeavor to encourage people to pray for the nations, believing firmly that prayer is far more powerful than guns or money.

We talked about the plan many times over the following year. Checking our schedules we found that mid-March looked good. We were both thinking of those who should join us. We agreed to let the Lord send people to us rather than recruiting them, for we wanted His team, not ours. So, each time we were with groups of people who were inclined to pray, we mentioned the trip and waited to see who the Lord would send.

Nearly 100 people began the personal process of wanting to come on this trip. I laughed to myself as I thought of it. The cell in which we were secreted would never have accommodated 100 people. How would the outcome have been different if they had all been sent?

Some could not clear the time for the trip. We had projected one month, but had said that people could join and leave the team at different dates. Those who like scuba-diving could join us for the Grand Canyon of Aceh, an underwater festival of marine life. Others could join us for the "Cross-Sumatra" trek which would take us from one side of this mountain in the sea to the other. Others could join us for the "Encourage the Christians" portion in which we planned to identify Christian Churches in Aceh and stand with them in solidarity. Others could join us for the "Future Development of Aceh" portion which involved meeting local leaders to find humanitarian ways in which to develop the region in education, medicine, and microeconomics.

We tried to make the trip a "possibility" for as diverse a group as possible. At the end of nine months we had two of the hundred who were still interested. They were the Doctor, a veteran of trips in Latin America and Asia, and a very trusted close personal friend, and the Banker. The Banker had wanted to spend a month in daily discipleship as he identified his mission for the second half of his life in Christ.

We agreed to meet in Singapore. Each of us had the backing of our families, our pastors, and the financial support we needed for the trip. We met, spent a few days getting used to the time zone, the climate and each other and made our way across the Straits of Malacca. We hired the car and driver in Medan and headed north. Our team included the Chinese, the Doctor, the Banker, and me. We spent a great deal of our time looking at schools, clinics, and small businesses, and developing a plan for microeconomic development based on our belief that the proceeds of the oil industry would not trickle down to the farmer and small business owner.

The sending of laymen to mission fields had been embraced by all denominations. We have facilitated short-term teams since 1976 and have enabled carpenters to rebuild ravaged villages, doctors to rebuild ravaged hearts, and loving compassionate people of all walks of life to rebuild ravaged people. Whether farmer or physiologist, tractor operator or teacher, people of all persuasions have enjoyed their experiences in serving those unable to help themselves. One of our more regular travelers has often said, "These two weeks each year add value to the rest of my year. When I go to work in the morning, I know that some part of my work this day will help one of these who have such great needs."

The pathway to a meaningful "vacation with a purpose" is very simple. It is easy to be sent. First, think about a group of people who have a need. You can research through the internet, through your church, through National Geographic Magazine, through universities or your employer. Many corporations have found a tremendous boost to employee morale by sponsoring a relief project or training project in a developing nation or region in their home country. Inform yourself of the opportunities.

Next, contact the organization working where you feel you would like to participate. The Banker and Doctor had contacted me through mutual friends. We had not anticipated spending our day being defended from an Irate Imam and his band of unhappy people; but, we certainly loved the local people and had the resource to be of benefit to them. You may want to contact us or another group. Think about it. Pray about it. Ask for information on the group and see if they will allow you to talk with someone who has been on one of their trips or projects. Be sure to ask, "Who pays?" during this step. Any answer other than "We do" is "You do."

Next, submit your idea to a trusted friend or to your supervisor, or to your Pastor or church leaders. Give them the opportunity to participate in your "sending." This gives you the emotional support necessary to overcome separation anxiety and allows them the opportunity to vicariously participate in your journey. One of our more frequent travelers owns an Auto Repair Shop. He takes pictures of every place he goes and makes albums for the waiting room of his garage. While people wait for their car they enjoy a soft drink or coffee and see where their money is going. He saves a percentage of every account in a special fund for his travels. The person paying a mechanic $55 per hour loves to see that children in Cambodia are eating because of their choice of garage. He has many notes from clients who are thrilled to participate with him in his newfound sense of worth.

Several years ago, the Melody Beauty Salon in Springdale, PA, was a major sponsor for child relief in Latin America. The ladies there donated a part of every account to finding and feeding kids. Certainly there were a few who stopped patronizing the place, but the vast majority of their ever-increasing clientele were touched to be able to sponsor travelers to meet the needs of the children.

Habitat for Humanity has set new horizons for people who want to do more than give money to projects. Now you can travel a short distance and get hot and sweaty for a good reason. The backing of Oprah and President Carter has lifted this "good idea" to a tangible, now global demonstration of love. By sharing their personal heartfelt desire to help people, Habitat has mobilized thousands of volunteers. Sharing your idea with others is not self exultant. Actually, it can be very humbling.

We four in our little cell were sent by thousands of people who share our common faith and understanding of the application of the faith to meet human need. We were not alone in our trial. We were not at all alone in that place. Because we had followed proper steps, there were people in Indonesia who knew our whereabouts. There were people in Singapore and every other nation of Asia who were tracking our daily progress. The Doctor had informed a network, as had the Banker, and I had 1,500 people praying daily for our trip.

Our families were definitely aware of where we were and what we were doing every day. The Doctor's wife and children, the Banker's wife and children, and my wife and sons were very much with us in spirit as we awaited the outcome of these events. But, even more present was the Holy Spirit.

Jesus is the One who sends us. He touches our hearts with a need. He continues to draw us to that need. He plants an idea in our minds concerning that need. He makes a pathway for our feet to get us to that need and He accompanies us to the location of that need. In the West we think of "Send" as "See you later." In the East we have a different understanding. Here, when someone says "We will send you," it means "We will go together." When Jesus said, "I send you as sheep among wolves," He meant He would be with us in the midst of the wolf pack.

When He sent the disciples "into all the earth to preach the gospel to all creatures, making disciples of the nations," He also said, "And I am with you even to the end of the age." As I sat in that cell with the "sent ones" I was very aware of the calm peace of the Lord. As the dusk gathered in corners of the cell, despair was driven away by a warm sense of the presence of God.

I thought we would die. In fact, I was fully persuaded of it. And, because of that peaceful presence, I was ready to see Jesus face to face. I knew He would meet the needs of my family. I had confidence that He would watch over them. I was, honestly, looking forward to seeing Him.

"A Faith to Die For"

Acts 1:4-8

⁴*And being assembled together with them, He commanded them not to depart from Jerusalem, but to wait for the Promise of the Father, "which," He said, "you have heard from Me;* ⁵*for John truly baptized with water, but you shall be baptized with the Holy Spirit not many days from now."* ⁶*Therefore, when they had come together, they asked Him, saying, "Lord, will You at this time restore the kingdom to Israel?"* ⁷*And He said to them, "It is not for you to know times or seasons which the Father has put in His own authority.* ⁸*But you shall receive power when the Holy Spirit has come upon you; and you shall be witnesses to Me[a] in Jerusalem, and in all Judea and Samaria, and to the end of the earth."*

Rev 12:10-12

¹⁰*Then I heard a loud voice saying in heaven, "Now salvation, and strength, and the kingdom of our God, and the power of His Christ have come, for the accuser of our brethren, who accused them before our God day and night, has been cast down.* ¹¹*And they overcame him by the blood of the Lamb and by the word of their testimony, and they did not love their lives to the death.* ¹²*Therefore rejoice, O heavens, and you who dwell in them! Woe to the inhabitants of the earth and the sea! For the devil has come down to you, having great wrath, because he knows that he has a short time."*

Where had this confidence come from?

Where had this confidence come from? Was I crazy, just trying to think of the ultimate escape, or was it a real confidence that would allow me to say as Leck had high in the hills of Thailand, "Father, I ask you to forgive him in Jesus' Name." I didn't know how it would come, whether we would be dragged into the street or shot in the cell and then the building burned. I had no idea if we would be the hooded captives shown on TV and used to extort money from the rational, or if we would just "disappear" as many trekkers do; but, I had the confidence that I would see Jesus.

Looking about the cell, my eyes met the Banker's. He was relaxed, poised, in deep thought as we all were. The crowd was really getting loud and it seemed that soon they would make the final rush that would overthrow the police and they would come crashing in to send us to our eternal rest. He held up nine fingers and shared with me a tense smile. Silence often says more than words ever could.

The Doctor looked at me and said, "I love my wife. I really love my wife. Oh God forgive me, I really love my wife." Pressure level nine causes men to repent of every nasty word they have ever said to the ones they love. Suddenly, mid-life crises are seen for the hopeless offers they extend.

The Chinese looked at each of us and, with typical Asian resolve, sat down to await the outcome. The arrival of the "Ninja," the "Interpol," and the "Officer" announced another briefing and situation update.

The "Officer" spoke for the group. "OK. We have come to a serious time in this operation. The commandoes are just a few minutes from arrival at the rear of the mob. They are expected, so there will be a battle there. They will quickly fight their way through to relieve us. We do not know which way the crowd will move. They may rush us. If they do, do not worry, we will protect you."

The "Ninja" picked it up from there. "We are going to close this metal door for your protection. Please do not open it for anyone. We are prepared for this. Please do not try to get out through any other way. Please remain calm."

Closing the door, we took our positions for what we all thought would be the last few minutes of our lives. The Banker and I stood by the door. The Doctor and the Chinese sat behind us. The Banker broke the tense silence, "This is a #10 situation." We had reached the top for a man with 243 Golden Glove bouts and three martial arts Black Belts. How does that compare to the experience level of a Doctor, a Missionary, and a machinist who just wanted to travel and pray for some people? Taking a deep breath, we prepared to meet our Creator.

In the moments that followed I thought of situations that the Lord had allowed to prepare me for this hour. They comforted me as I awaited the inevitable crash of the wave of the multitude-turned-mob on the shore of public safety maintaining order.

✳✳✳

IN the summer of 1978, I was walking door to door in the Guatemalan village of Zacualpa, Quiché. This municipality was the seat of government for 12,000 people, mostly the Quiché branch of the Mayan peoples. For some reason yet to be explained by anthropologists, these tribes had left their jungle habitat at Tikal and had fled to the mountains. I was there at the request of a development group to see if we thought that they would be receptive to medical, agricultural, and educational development. They were, and as a first step I was going from house to house to give a Bible to anyone who could read Spanish. This was our way of sharing the good news of Jesus and determining a reading level for the development of educational projects. We were finding one child in a family of as many as eight people who could read. The rural schools were expensive and, in the Mayan thought of family, each person has a responsibility to share whatever they learn with the others in an evening family circle.

I stood in front of an elaborate adobe structure at about 10 am and was preparing to knock on the door when a little boy took my arm and said, "Uncle, could you please follow me?"

Following him I entered a hovel of straw, mat, walls, dirt floor, and plastic roof. There stood his mother, grandmother, older and younger sisters. I began to share with him about the Bible and to make the customary inquiries about his reading ability.

Interrupting he pointed my attention to a man sleeping on a wooden door on the floor at the back corner of the hovel. He asked if I would pray for the man. I did, touching only the flannel sleeve of his shirt, not wanting to interrupt what must have been a very deep repose.

Having prayed, I turned back to the little group. We were just establishing the fact of the older sister's reading ability when, once again, the boy interrupted. This time he opened his mouth to speak, but no words came out. His eyes grew big as saucers staring at something behind me. Thinking it was a spider, snake, or scorpion I turned just in time to see the man on the door wake up, stretch, roll over and go back to sleep.

Thinking little of it, I finished the Bible presentation and continued toward my goal of 17 new readers for the day. The afternoon went well until I was handed a note telling me to leave the town or be killed. I took it to the police to see if it was real and they asked me to leave, saying that they could not protect me. This was the work of the Army of the Poor.

I left and worked in another region of Guatemala for the next six months. We had no computers or email in those late seventies, so I was not surprised to receive a hand delivered Telex. The content was a bit surprising as I was being invited to return to that town to speak. I checked with the police and military to see if it was alright to go. Six pastors had been killed; one a month, in the passing time.

The police assured me that it was alright to go, so I got a ride with a mission aviator and landed, to be met by a group of people who took me to the same adobe home. After a dinner of beans and rice we were joined by a throng of people. The furniture was pushed aside and people filled the room. I stood against the wall and looked out the window frame to see hundreds of people around the house. To my inquiry of the situation my host replied.

"Do you see that man over there?" He indicated a mid-thirties gentleman across the room.

"Yes," I said, "What about him?"

"Do you remember him? He lived in a hovel behind my place. He had a small family. You went there and prayed for him."

"Oh yes." Now I remembered. "Glad to see he is alright."

"You do not understand," my host continued. "He was dead. His body was lying there waiting for the wake.

These people have come to hear you because of this miracle. That is why the Army of the Poor had to get rid of you. The people were no longer afraid of them because they felt you would also raise them from the dead."

I was amazed. I had no idea the man was dead. If I had known I would have offered condolences to the family and bid a hasty farewell.

***

Standing now on the "safe side" of a metal door in the darkness of an unlit cell, I began to again feel the presence of the One who has the power over death. I could hear the sound of the battle outside and wondered how many would die that evening.

Looking at the Doctor, the Banker, and the Chinese, I wondered who would be the first to die. Would they just roll a grenade into the cell and kill us all? Probably not, the mass graves told the story of extreme butchery and savage torture.

These friends of mine were so peaceful. There was no panic, no argument, and no accusation. I could see that the confident peace and assurance of hope was theirs as well. We were ready to meet Jesus. Each one of us had a certain anticipation of the moment we would face Him having died in His service.

I could suddenly hear the sounds of battle as the commando-driven mob had made their rush on the building and the firefight had reached the interior hallway. There were the sounds of gunfire and men calling to each other. I was too preoccupied to even consider moving from the door. The Banker was equally focused, leaning forward toward the door, he was positioning himself for defense should it suddenly spring open.

"Why had the stuffed T-shirt mentioned Ambon?" The question flew into my mind like a bullet careening through the hallway. Ambon had been lovely before the Irate Imams inflamed the people against the Christians.

The gem

AMBON is the gem of the Malluku Islands about a thousand miles from where we awaited our destiny. Walking there had been a delight. The oil-rich area was home to docile people groups who spent their lives working for the development of the island paradise. I had traveled there at the request of a national Christian movement to teach on prayer. Hosted by a former national director for A&W Root Beer, an American fast food chain, I had thoroughly enjoyed the fellowship of their fledgling church.

Ambon was one of those places to which the Java government had sent denizens of their overcrowded cities. These had come from the Southern tip of the island of Sumatra and for the most part were from a very radical Moslem people group, the Madurese. Their native island of Madura was known as a place in which seven Christian churches had been burned. I had also been there and had interviewed the oldest-ranking Christian who had explained to me that a faith which allows four wives and encourages many children, will eventually displace a faith that allows one wife and suggests family planning. His church had grown in previous generations through large families.

His church and everything in it had been burned to the ground two years before. He had complained to the government in Jakarta and they had provided the money to rebuild. However, the point had been made and he and his followers knew that at any moment they could be taken to the church and burned alive as others had been.

This same group, the Madurese, had shifted to Surabaya and, finding a ghetto teeming with malaria and dysentery, had again relocated to the sweet breezes of Ambon. There it was just a matter of time before their population would become dominant in the democratic process and law would become Shariah or Islamic code.

The place was filled with teenagers. I watched the city basketball team practice and again saw how sport could unify rather than divide. Pointed toward a common goal, these young men left their religion behind and cooperated in a most polished way. I was really impressed with the way they moved the ball. Their anticipation of each other's location on the court spoke of hours of training together. The idea that an Inflamed Imam could ever ignite a fanatic frenzy that would pit one of these youth against another was beyond my belief.

After practice the team had attended a youth rally in which I spoke of Jesus' impartial love for all and our need for impartial love for one another. They all responded to prayer, Christian and Moslem alike. These young people humbled themselves before God and asked that unity and love prevail in their community. There was not one hint of racial or religious tension in the place.

Ambon had been known for two beautiful structures, one of which was the Islamic Mosque dating to the fourteenth century. Its emerald grandeur had attracted me from the moment I arrived in town. When I visited it, I just sat for an hour or so and thought through the history of

Islam in the islands that would one day become the Republic of Indonesia. Certainly there had been "conversions" to Islam, but the strategy implemented in most cases had been to populate, propagate, and dominate. This was the same in the US states of Michigan and New Jersey. This Mosque, set on a hill on the eastern side of the city had been a center for the domination of the region. Its minarets of beautifully fashioned local hardwood were majestic. From their towering height prayers were broadcast into the bustling valley below.

Opposite and about two miles across the city was the Dutch Reformed Cathedral. Equally grand in a European statement of colonialism not unlike the Arab, its white steeple rose high above the valley population. The town rested in the peaceful relationship of these twin towers. The commercial center was developed by the Chinese who had come to the region in the fifteenth century. They were interested only in serving the needs of the other groups and making money. Their simply-stated temple was to the god of prosperity. They just wanted peace and, in typical Chinese fashion, lived austere lives while amassing fortunes for future generations. There, five avenues of shops provided everything from stereos to steam engines. The Arab, Chinese, European, and local cultures had worked in unity to create an absolutely beautiful example of how good life can be.

Then it happened. Police reports are inconclusive concerning the spark that ignited the flame that burned the commercial center to the ground and sent thousands of these youth to their graves. Some say it was an offense over a relationship between a Moslem boy and a Christian girl. Others say that the population had reached an exact balance of Moslem and non-Moslem and the non-Moslems started the fight to try to drive out the Madurese settlers.

Others said it was "outsiders," sent to disrupt the harmony of the place. Whatever the combination of logs thrown on the fire, the heat was intense. In one action reported to me by an eyewitness, children on a Sunday school outing were suddenly surrounded by a mob of Moslem youth led by a man in his forties. One of the children, a boy of seven, was held by the larger boys and told to deny Christ and declare the Prophet. When he refused, a machete flew threw the air and removed his right arm. Again he was told to reject Christ and declare the Prophet. He again refused and the machete cut off his left leg below the knee. Caught up in the frenzy of mutilation, the youth allowed the other children to flee into the forest and continued to decimate the seven-year-old.

The horror-stricken children ran to their homes and told their parents of the incident and enraged adults took to the street. Months passed as thousands died in the bloodshed. When troops dispatched to cool the violence could not, they became the target of both Moslem and Christian mobs. The battles raged night and day. The Christians defended the Cathedral, the Moslems defended the mosque and the buildings of the Chinese merchants who fled the region were burned and looted. At the last, the twin towers stood over a field of bloodshed and destruction.

There was only one place left that was not totally covered with the rubble of ruin. In the center of what had been a beautiful city, the pride of the islands, the gem stone of the wedding ring of the Indonesian marriage of peoples, was the basketball court. There was no sound of team-mate calling to team-mate. There was no team. They had been distracted to become the precise opposite of what they had dreamed. Fueled by rhetoric, ignited by adults, these youth had turned against each other.

What had that stuffed T-shirt meant with his declaration, "This is not Ambon." And why had his frightened friend stood there in distress as from under the baseball cap had spewed forth the words, "This is my friend, he is a "Christian." Why had the tone not matched the words? Why had the face not reflected the faith? Why had the 'Christian' not said one word?

Things were heating up again outside the metal door. We could hear the sounds of fighting in the building and realized it would be just a moment before someone prevailed. From the cheering of the crowd, we felt that it was not all going our way. Blinded by the rusting panel before us and not at all certain of its protective power, I watched the Banker prepare for battle. He flexed his hands and made certain his footing.

How would they do it, this frenzied mob? Would they take one of us and try to get us to deny our faith for their amusement? Would they take us to some jungle camp and keep us there for years till our families assumed us dead? Would they use us as pawns in a negotiation with Jakarta for the release of their brothers held prisoner?

I knew that the United States Government would not negotiate. Our ministry would not negotiate; we had no money to pay and would not ask any of our donors to put up the money. The others had some resource, but these people would ask for millions or for political concessions and neither of those was going to happen. I hoped they would just throw open the door and kill us all with a burst of automatic weapons fire. I fully expected to watch it happen as our spirits left our bodies for our heavenly home.

The persuasions of life and death wrestled in my mind. On the one hand I would suffer death in this cell. On the other hand, I would see Jesus face to face. At what point would the Holy Spirit lift me from the situation? How much pain would I feel? Could the Lord arrange a quick exit from this life or would He need a testimony to be spoken? How much grace could be drawn from the future hope that was in us? How real was our salvation?

Jesus had endured the cross looking forward to the hope that lay before Him. Would we have three hours, three days, three weeks, three years? What would our lot be? All of these questions raced through my adrenaline-enriched mind. The Banker was cool, set for action, poised.

CHAPTER TWENTY-ONE

What ultimately controls a mob of people?

W HAT ultimately controls a mob of people? Is the blood frenzy abated at the sacrifice of an individual? Is it the arrival of a uniformed mob whose strength is perceived to be greater? In Ambon the uniforms became a focal point of common hatred. I suppose in their deaths they were a sacrifice that abated some of the poisoned passions.

What would it take for these several thousands of fanatic forces to leave off their drives of passion and hatred and walk away from four Christian testimonies waiting to be offered? In some cases, they like to play cat and mouse, offering peace and then striking the individual. Would they tie us in a row and march us through the town as trophies, a declaration of their superior manhood over the Java government and the United States?

No seven-year-old here, would they strike down the one they perceived to be the emotionally weakest and mutilate him before the others? Would they show preference to the Chinese, not wanting to deal with a neighboring government for the consequence? I determined that when the door finally opened I would step in front of the others. It wasn't gallantry; I really could feel the presence of the Lord and was equipped by Him to take the hit. It is a rule in our groups that the leader takes the hit, whether it is arrest, or physical; we do not stand back or run from a situation.

Clothed in robes of righteousness, I was ready to see the Lord. I thought very quickly of the 25 years of ministry with Him. I thought of my salvation experience, of my Christian heritage, of the faith of my parents and those with whom they fellowshipped. If, at the age of 51, the Lord had determined that I was ready to be offered, then so be it.

In those moments I thought of a martyr who had gone before. He had been a family man with three little children. His nation of Laos was caught in the dawning reality of the decline of communism and the emergence of a capitalistic, free-market economy. The residual hatred of the United States for its use of chemicals during the Vietnam War had scarred the people to the extent that they hated anything associated with America. His receiving of and preaching of the gospel of Jesus Christ had landed him in a Lao jail.

His wife and three children had awaited his release, but in the flu season she had become very ill and had passed away. When informed of this, the government agreed to release the father to the three children if he would "sign out." That is to say sign a document saying that his conversion had been coerced and that he had really not understood what he was doing.

On the day appointed, he signed out and was released. The children, having buried their mother, came to collect there father. He was released and they walked happily through the jail yard to the gate which was opened for them. As they walked down the street, a man walked up to them, produced a pistol, and began to shoot their father. The final killing round was at close range. The oldest child, a daughter, attempted to shield her father's head with her hand and the man shot right through her hand to kill her father. This is terror. This is a statement meant to be communicated to others as I am communicating it to you. These are the prices people pay every day around the world for the crime of saying, "I believe Jesus Christ is the Son of God."

What price would we pay that Aceh day?

The shooting stopped. The "Banker" and I were face to face, our shoulders to the door. We could smell the gun smoke; we could hear moans in the hall. We looked at each other and awaited our fate.

There was a knock on the door and a voice, "Open the door."

Remembering the instruction and with the "Banker's" agreement I slid open the little sliding metal strip. Our eyes met through the space. Was he my executioner or my deliverer? Was he the one sent of God to dispatch me from the affairs of this life, or was he the one who would throw a hood over my head, beat me for awhile and then drag me as a trophy to the waiting mob?

"Open the door." His persuader was a large automatic weapon.

Looking at the others for agreement, we stepped back and opened the door.

He stood and looked at us. The weapon was hot and heavy in his hand as he lowered the barrel toward us. His face was streaked with sweat and dirt; his eyes were filled with the sights of combat. He stared at me and said, "Are you Mr Mark?"

"Yes," I answered, focusing on the gun barrel.

"Are you a Christian?"

Ah, the question that can take you to heaven. I was ready to go. Past fear, past thoughts of torture, resigned to whatever fate the Lord had for me and selected from the group, bolstered by the ever-increasing sense of the presence of a loving God, with hope alive in my heart, I said, "Yes, I am."

I was ready to go. All issues resolved. Peace in my heart. Absence of fear. I was ready to see Jesus. I had heard His voice. I had felt His hand upon me. I had walked with Him among the nations. I had seen Him raise the dead. I had known his great comfort.

Now I was going to see Him face to face and say, "Thank You."

I was ready. He was there just as He had promised He would be.

"Catholic or Protestant?" The question was out of the picture.

What a crazy question to ask a man who is ready to see Jesus. Who cares? Just do whatever you are sent here to do and let's get on with it. Man, I could see myself with Peter, James, John, and the others who had given their life for Christ. I was ready for the front row in heaven. I was prepared by the Holy Spirit to enter into eternal reward, dispatched from the earth by this young gunman. What a crazy question to ask a man who is ready to go.

"Protestant," I answered as I felt the hope leaving and reality settling in.

"So am I," he said. "Stay here, we have some cleaning up to do and then someone will come for you. Get down and crawl along the hall. It is dark. Take his hand and he will lead you. There are many people here who want to kill you, so please stay down."

With that he left, we got down, and looked at each other. A quick smile was all we could manage as the tension of the moment had left each of us drained. Within a few moments another person came. Following the instructions we crawled through the hall and clambered over the seats of a travel-all that had been backed up to the charred door of the jail house. An armed commando sat down atop each of us and pressed us into the floor boards. They were very polite, professional and uncompromising in their instruction for us to keep our heads down.

I lifted my head to capture the moment in a memory that shall never pass. The building had been burned. Our car had been burned, and next to it was a police car which had suffered the same fate. A military truck was parked there, the windows smashed out and the metal showing the scars of attack. Another truck was parked in front of our vehicle to obstruct the view of the mob.

They were on the other side of the street. The "Ninja" stood before them, a large automatic perched on his hip watching for any who would try to again cross the road or throw anything.

Three commandos approached our vehicle. One took the wheel and another, the front passenger seat; the third went to the truck to move it for our exit.

"Get on the floor, keep your heads down, and do not lift your heads up no matter what happens." The orders came from the passenger seat.

"Are you Mr. Mark?" he asked, looking at me.

"Yes," I answered.

"One of my men died for you today. He took a bullet through his eye ..."

"Quiet!" barked the In-Charge, who was driving. "He is not to know."

Feeling devastated and increasingly aware of the desperate situation through which we had come, I settled into the floorboards and thanked the Lord for being alive.

Through the night we sped. We were four very happy Christian men being swept through the warm tropical evening in a military convoy. After about 20 minutes we were allowed to sit up. For the first time we could see the faces of those who had come to save us. They were very professional. Eyes to the front, they did not say a word. With the passing of the miles, we began to realize the situation was not over, it was just changing location.

We arrived at a military base and were escorted to a large sitting room. The Lieutenant was very young. He introduced himself as our translator. Then he offered a synopsis of our situation. We had walked into a very tense political confrontation. Handing out Christian Literature would be blamed for the resultant demonstration; but, in actual fact something else was going on. He was not authorized to explain, but we were to wait here at this facility for our safety and for an investigation of the events.

We had not seen our passports, so I asked if we were under arrest. He said to think of it as "protective custody" and he would let me know if and what charges would be filed against us.

My three friends walked about to survey the building in which we would be kept for the next few days. I sat back in the soft chair and thanked the Lord for leaving me here. I had been ready to go, but the thought of rejoining my wife and kids was suddenly more important. The Lieutenant cautioned us about going outside or standing in front of the glass doors. They were concerned that if we were found to be at this station an even greater mob would gather and use our presence to justify attacking this post.

As the others stretched their legs, I sat with this young man.

"What actually happened there?" I asked.

"I cannot tell you," he answered. "Just pay attention to the types of questions they ask and you will be able to figure it out."

"I understand you are a Christian." His eyes met mine.

"Yes, I am." It just didn't have the same feel as it had in the cell.

"So am I," he offered. "I was posted here because I am a believer. There are two of us in this unit. The other is the Commander. That will not help your situation; but, before this all begins I want you to know that we are extremely proud of the four of you."

CHAPTER TWENTY-TWO

The days passed slowly

THE days passed slowly. We slept on the tile floor of the conference room. We were constantly under guard. The air-conditioning was on freezing and we had to pay US currency to use the toilet. We were taken for questioning at any time, day or night, and with a variety of individuals ranging from friendly to antagonistic.

My first session started at midnight the night of our rescue. I followed the Lieutenant's suggestion and listened closely to the questions. I was at first completely disarmed by the fact that the man asking the questions was the same fellow behind whom I had crawled out of the cell. He was now in plain clothes, chain smoking and leaning in on me. Accompanied by four or five alternating scribes he pressed into my space.

After we had cleared the initial steps of information readily available from my passport and after my questions concerning our arrest had been completely ignored, he leaned in and shouted, "You are CIA!"

Amazed, I sat back in the chair, but the people behind me put their arms across the back pressing me forward into his cigarette smoke, foul stench, and loud accusation.

"You are CIA and I am going to prove it." He looked very fierce, this deliverer turned accuser.

"What makes you think I am CIA?" I asked. After the pressure we went through, this was almost humorous. I have no idea what a CIA person is like, but I am definitely not, nor ever have been one. If he meant Christian In Action, of course; but I am not associated with any US Government Agency and our foundation receives no money from any Government.

"Yes," he shouted into my face, "You are CIA and I am going to prove it."

"You had better stop chain smoking or you are going to die a very slow death of cancer in the lungs which will spread through your body and kill you," I answered.

Looking at his fifth cigarette he asked if I knew how he could quit. His abandoning of the CIA issue was a relief. His heart was not really in this session. I think he just wanted to get to bed. It had been a long pressure-filled day and this young man needed some rest.

"What makes you think I am CIA?" I asked.

"Your age, your haircut, your glasses, and your watch, and the place where you were. And," he continued, "You are not afraid of me."

"Afraid of you?" I asked. "I was going to be killed and you came and saved me. Why would I be afraid of you?"

"Look," he said. "You were in the wrong place at the wrong time. You all look very well-trained. You, especially, stay very cool under pressure. The other one walks like a cat. The Chinese has no nerves. And the other American talks nonstop. You look to us like a trained team."

Then I realized what had happened. We had all reverted to our previous training. We had all served in the military. We had been prepared for what to do in the event of capture and we were doing it. Instead of being a group of missionaries who had been trained to kneel down and accept the inevitable, we were fine-tuned to the situation and the people in it. This gave the impression to the military/police types that we were on a mission. My guy thought I was not afraid because I was staring into his right eye when he talked to me. We were trained to do it and I had just slipped back into the training of so many years before.

By 2 am he had had enough of this. Tired from a very emotional day he had me escorted to the room in which we stayed. Once reunited we gave thanks to the Lord for our safety, prayed for our families, and got a bit of sleep before the next day's round of questions.

The process continued for three days before the final questioning. The police brought in a group of "teachers." We were instructed to cooperate fully with them, telling them every detail of who we were and why we were there. During the night, the Banker had managed to get a call out to his wife. He had simply ripped the plastic cover from an office phone and made the call. She had called her Pastor and he had called the US Embassy in Jakarta to find our whereabouts.

We refused to give any further information saying that they had a signed statement from us and that was all they needed. "Charge us with a crime, or let us go" was our agreed-upon position and we boldly refused to cooperate.

They went and got the commander to persuade me to change our course.

I explained to him that we were showing signs of cracking emotionally under their method of questioning. We really had nothing to hide. We were not lying to them or covering any point. I asked him if we could please make this the last day of this process, evaluate the testimonies and do whatever he had to do to move us back to our homes. I pressed the point that we had broken no law in Indonesia, any loss of property or damages was the result of Indonesian with Indonesians, and though we were very sorry for any part we had played, we needed to move on.

He was very happy that we would cooperate and gave me his word that he would do all he could to expedite the process. And so, we entered the last full day of questioning.

They put me in one room with the former chain smoker. Now every time he reached for a cigarette, I reached across the table and took it from him. He was really trying. I told him that what had worked for me was to call the name of Jesus every time I wanted another cigarette. So, there he was calling on the name of the Lord while I was being questioned.

We had a new interviewer. A distinguished gentleman in his sixties, he started off in a very friendly fashion. His English was quite good and I basically liked him. Their plan was to get a statement from me and then try to confirm or contradict it by calling one of the others and asking them the same key questions.

The man began by asking me to tell him how I grew up, all of my education, any military service, what I did for a living, and why I was in Aceh during those days.

I took him step by step through the process of being born in a Christian family, having the Children's Bible as my first book, having perfect Sunday School attendance, morning and evening family devotions, the impact of David Wilkerson and Kathryn Kuhlman, being a Teen Youth Leader, and then the rebellion years as the faith became my own.

He sat spell-bound as I told him the step-by-step process of Christian growth, the significance of the Bible, prayer, and fellowship in forming young lives.

After a break for coffee and toilet, we again walked the road of testimony. Together we traveled through early college years and then the military, then the release from active duty, marriage to a Christian girl, rededication to Christ and the business years.

We broke for lunch, a first for us. And then step by step we walked the path of the call of God to preach to the nations, return to school for preparation, the early years in missions, the development of missions in a local church, the creation of a Bible School, the training of others to take the good news, and the eventual founding of South East Asia Prayer Center (SEAPC). At no point were they bored by or antagonistic to the story. The former chain smoker took notes of all that I said.

When other officers entered with a specific question about our being there or where we got the materials we had given out, my man brushed them aside. He was enthralled with the testimony he was hearing.

At about 3 pm we came to the present situation. I explained that we were a team of four: a Foundation President, a Doctor, a Banker, and a local Chinese who served as our guide. We were traveling in Aceh to see if there was any platform from which SEAPC could become involved in humanitarian efforts. Because we were taking photos of clinics, schools, farms, homes, and other personal property, we had desired to have a gift to give to the people to cover our intrusion. The books and cassettes had come from a friend of a friend and, since freedom of religion was guaranteed by the constitution of the Republic of Indonesia, we felt free to give these as a "thank you."

He was amazed at my testimony. He said, "Mark, I would like to thank you for sharing so openly with me. I am a Moslem, born in a Moslem family. I have never heard the step by step testimony of a Christian born in a Christian family. Now, I understand so much more of the way you think and the faith you have.

"Aceh will be a free republic soon. Our representatives are in Geneva and will meet with those of your government. They have already agreed to recognize us as a country once these hostilities are over.

"When that happens I will be a leader in the new Aceh. Would you then come back and help us to develop our nation? We need medicine, education, and economic development and I would like to invite you to return."

"I would be delighted," I responded realizing that this was little more than the customary Indonesian apology at the end of what could have been a distasteful exchange. "But, could I ask you a question?"

"Certainly, what would you like to know?" He sat relaxed as did the others in the room.

"Why did you think we were CIA?" They were a bit taken aback by my candor.

From furtive glances came the answer. "We were told that the action that would drive the Java government from Aceh was to begin that afternoon. When you four came to the police station, the people thought that you were a team of CIA agents sent to take out the station from within. They started the riot to cover for you. When the station was not taken, they decided that you all had broken promise and they took the situation in their own hands."

Was it disinformation? Was it the truth? Administrations have changed. 911 has happened. Exxon/Mobil has negotiated a new deal with Aceh. Who knows for sure what went on that March afternoon. Many times I have thought back through the step-by-step events of the day. We have discussed it among the four of us; comparing the questions we were asked. I saw the Banker in China, I have traveled again with the Chinese, and the Doctor and his wife are again walking hand in hand.

We kept in touch with the Lieutenant even though the

following morning we were photographed, finger-printed, charged with being missionaries on a tourist visa, arraigned, tried, convicted, handed over to Immigration Police, escorted to the city of Medan, blacklisted from Indonesia and put on a plane to Singapore.

Recently, *The Economist* ran an article referring to the Straits of Malacca and the flow of oil from the Gulf to Japan, Taiwan, Korea and other markets. The writer referred to Aceh as the key to the whole plan. When I saw the article I thought you, the reader, might like to read this book. As events unfold in their step-by-step adventure to globalization, you should know about the "stuffed T-shirt," "the Ninja," and the "Interpol" and a group of four who have seen it face to face.

Where does a person's faith fit in a globalized economy? Is this the new economic deliverer of the oppressed? Are we really to believe that the youthful "multitude" in a dusty demonstration in Aceh are going to find hope for their futures in a free trade agreement or a globalized economy? Is their hope to be based on a society without personal belief? If they are persons of religious discipline, will they have to take up rockets, grenades, land mines, and missiles to further that belief?

And, what if they become "Sent Ones?" Will that mean Arab Militia or Mounted Cavalry? There are already "martyrs" becoming "suicide bombers." Are they heroes in the struggle for freedom from oppression or are they pawns in the new surge toward uniting all under one banner?

CHAPTER TWENTY-THREE

The times have changed

THE times have changed. Now the world is feeling the impact known just a few years ago by a handful of people in remote places like Aceh and Ambon. The Jihad or Holy War has spread around the globe. Even in the aftermath of 911, places like Spain and Turkey have replaced Manhattan in the headlines. But, what of the little village people who live every day in the fear of a sudden attack? What of the multitudes who try to find hope in refugee camps until it becomes clear that they have been forgotten? What of the unfortunate women and children who happened to get caught up in last night's precision bombing who, with the clear light of day, have neither health nor home?

We endure the headlines of today's latest bomb blast and UN debate and rush to see how the markets have done, or what the price of crude is. We have become desensitized so that an "Arab Militia" making widows and orphans in the Sudan is a "humanitarian crisis" and not a "genocide." From Dearborn, Michigan, to Durban, South Africa, we have learned to say the right thing, do the right thing, and to keep from upsetting the latest global bully.

Jesus saw the multitude and they were like sheep without a shepherd. He promised to feed His flock like a shepherd and to carry the lambs in His own arms. To the Christian, He is the Lamb become Lion, the Prophet King. To the Moslem He is the coming Judge of the World; He is a prophet to be obeyed.

He said to the Palestinian woman at the well, "Anyone who drinks of these waters will never thirst again." She believed His words and went to what is now Nablus and told the others and the whole city came out to believe in Him. Her action resulted in eternal life for those who had been hoping something would happen to change their lowly status.

Among His disciples were fishermen and public servants. Even the Roman given the task of His execution declared, "Truly He is the Son of God." Greeks, Romans, Jews, Arabs, Africans, and Asians have found love for former enemies by embracing the Son of Love, Jesus Christ. He is the One who has torn down the wall of partition so that in Him there is neither Jew nor Greek; Barbarian nor Scythian; male nor female; slave nor free; but we are all one in Christ. The bonds of love form multi-ethnic, multi-lingual teams that travel the earth demonstrating the message of the Master through acts of kindness and self sacrifice.

He sends them. They are not self motivated. Often they find themselves in places they would not naturally go. They are mixed in color, mixed in background, but common in faith, hope and love. The people in the places to which they are sent see the love, find the hope, and come to the faith.

Some will not be well received. They will be persecuted. Some of them will die as those who seek to control the multitude do not want to relinquish that control. Therein is the conflict we found in Aceh. There was an agenda. Some other drama was being played out on the stage. I have often wondered if a travel-all with three Westerners and a Chinese arrived in town after we did, saw the situation, and drove on north. I suppose I shall never know, but love won the day.

Now, as I sit in Tibet five years after the "Aceh Incident" as it has come to be called, I wonder about a lot of things. The chain smoker made the connection to the New Hope. I have had contact with him. The last interrogator has also begun to follow the disciplines of Christ and is preparing to demonstrate His love through action for the people. The Lieutenant kept in touch for more than a year and was growing strong in grace when last we communicated. The United States has had an Administration change and with it has become embroiled in Jihad. Free Aceh is still negotiating in exile in Geneva and young people are still dying in Paradise.

I cannot return to Indonesia at this moment. I headed north from there and found a wonderful open door in Tibet. Now working as a guest of the government that thrice asked me to leave, we are bringing health care to children. A delay in government process has allowed me to write these things down for you. I hope you have enjoyed the faith and love you have found on these pages.

Christian growth and experience are not a "Once in a Lifetime" proposition. They are a step-by-step process. As we follow in the footsteps of Jesus, we find Him to be the giver of faith, the giver of Hope, and the giver of all love. He just gets "sweeter and sweeter as the days go by."

I hope our paths connect through this book. There are so many widows and fatherless children on the earth. They really need hope. As the religions argue over oil rights and weapons of mass destruction, let us be examples of what

James calls "pure religion and undefiled." Let us bring hope to this multitude of millions who, herded by war, disease, and natural disaster are truly "sheep without a shepherd."